This book is dedicated to my hero, Teresa Morton, who never compromised for the animals, along with Cheryl Gilmore, whose spirit and utter disregard for what people thought, made great strides for animal welfare by bringing attention to the thousands upon thousands of unwanted animals. It is also with great love and respect I must mention Anita Paddock, my mentor, along with Pam Pearce, my editor. I want to thank the Borderliners, my critique group, who made me tougher and put a little hair on my chest. I am also grateful for my husband and my dog, who put up with me.

Characters and events in this novel – even those based on real people – are entirely **fictional**.

FIXED: A TAIL OF A DOG

Tessa Freeman

Dogs never bite me. Just humans. --- Marilyn Monroe

Summer

Lily-Chapter 1

The Man with the Hole in His Smile tossed Lily in a cage with The Big Black Dog, who, lying motionless and twitching his stubby tail, stared at his empty food bowl. Lily looked around her. What was this terrible place? Lily wondered if she should introduce herself to The Big Black Dog, but he didn't seem that interested.

She thought about her brothers and sisters and how they had all played together in the grass and wondered if The Big Black Dog might enjoy a tussle. But that was a long time ago--before The Man with Kind Eyes had taken Lily from her litter mates.

She looked at her pretty tail, a white tuft at the end. It was much better than his at keeping the flying, biting things away. Hers was also cuter and much thinner. He had a thick stubby tail like a black sausage.

Thinking he might enjoy a game of tail tag like she used to play with her brothers and sisters, Lily took a deep breath and planted her spotted nose into The Big Black Dog's backside.

Suddenly, Lily saw two white fangs heading straight for her and ducked her fine head just in time to watch The Big Black Dog skid on his back and crash into the side of the kennel, his legs flailing in the air.

Frantically, Lily tried to corral her thoughts, it not taking too long, there so few of them. Lily would smile.

That would convince him to be her friend. After all, The Man with Kind Eyes had liked it when Lily had smiled at him.

But as The Big Black Dog pushed himself up on his spindly legs, Lily became frightened, her little legs quaking under her tiny body.

A loud crash rattled the kennels causing mutts of all makes to jump and bark. The Big Black Dog, his hind legs bounding out from under him, the toes of his forepaws wrapped around the thin steel-gauge wire of his kennel, was acting as much of a fool as the others.

Thus Lily decided she didn't want to be his friend anyway.

Tucking her pretty tail under her and sitting down, Lily cooly licked her paws, a trick she had learned from her old buddy, Tom, The Yellow-Striped Skinny Dog that she had known a long time ago.

Morgan-Chapter 2

 The heavy door slammed behind Morgan McAfee after she turned the key in the lock of McAfee Mutts Animal Shelter and walked through the threshold. Morgan wondered if this was the right place for an animal shelter, if they had chosen the location wisely.
 The rescue was in the middle of the city limits of Multown, Oklahoma, a small town that didn't amount to much. Yet it did lay claim to being the home of a former Miss America, a fact that made the city officials so proud that they named, in the beauty queen's honor, a strip of old Highway 64,

the little town's main street running through its middle-section. Now, at the turn of the twenty-first century, the four-lane highway, pock-marked and weather-beaten, teetered between adult video stores and quick cash exchanges littering Multown's flat horizon.

Cruel nature had been calling the shots in Morgan McAfee's life, which had become an endless haze of homeless dogs, usually with some malady, one after another. She couldn't even keep their colors straight anymore. The browns were melting into the blacks. The blacks into the grays. Life had become one big brindle.

McAfee Mutts was in a former nursing home that had been the town's sole elder care facility. It had been forced to shut down when a resident smoked a cigarette that burned down much of the building along with her. The owner, who had been sued by the deceased woman's family and needed money, sold the cement-block building to Morgan and her husband for a song.

"Yes, if one should want a nursing home," Ray, her husband, a dentist, would respond, making no bones about the fact that he didn't want to own a nursing home, though he often joked Morgan worked him hard enough to put him in one.

Ray spent most of his time transforming the former nursing home into an animal shelter while also running his Multown dental practice. Morgan had been his receptionist and office manager for thirty-four years since they met when she, as a teenager, walked into his office and applied for the job.

Where once-slobbering old people had played bingo, drooling dogs lived in twelve-by-twelve-by-twelve kennels made of steel-gauge wire, two in each of the six rooms that comprised one wing. The other two wings were in the process of being remodeled to eventually house the dogs ready and waiting to be adopted.

"But the dogs don't drool near as much as the old people did," Morgan would say, defending her dream of an orphaned dog utopia, the purchase of the old folks home just the beginning.

To try to stop the barking from making its way to the neighbors, Morgan had nailed blankets across the interior window facings. The mean old neighbor, the man with a rotting leg from diabetes who lived nearby and rolled around in an automated wheelchair, complained at the Multown City Council meetings about the noise. Since the little town in eastern Oklahoma had no city ordinance governing noise, it wasn't really a violation. Yet he complained just the same to Morgan who agreed it wasn't getting any quieter.

The homeless dogs just kept pouring in, more and more every day, with little space and money to take care of them. Morgan also ran the city pound, which she had assumed the responsibility for two years ago, without much help from Multown except for a dogcatcher paid for by the city.

They had just moved the dogs into the nursing home from the former city pound, comprised of outdoor pens and a precariously close proximity to a sewage pool on the edge of Multown. The volunteers, much to their dismay, had had to fish a few of the loose dogs out of the muck, especially the water dogs who were prone to take a swim.

But Morgan was determined the town wouldn't ever run the pound again. She had found dogs frozen to death in their doghouses and dead dogs in trash cans. It was up to her to make a better life for these abandoned animals, although moving the animals into the makeshift shelter was ahead of her plan. It was an expensive, difficult learning process. And, during the worst summer on record for eastern Oklahoma, it was one hot mess.

Parvovirus had just invaded McAfee Mutts, and as much as Morgan tried to fight it, she was somewhat relieved that the harsh arbiter of fate was making up her mind as to which dog would die next.

As she walked through the shelter, the dogs barking wildly, Morgan tried not to think about the eight little furry bodies, now frozen solid, inside the freezer.

She had put them to sleep the night before and wondered if the dog catcher had already come to dispose of them. Morgan envisioned him tossing the carcasses by their frozen legs into a trash bag then throwing the bag over his back. He would have lumbered down the wide hall toward the heavy security-glass door, ignoring the forty-nine eyes peering at him. His heavy breath would have whistled through his tooth gap.

He might have wondered what he would have for lunch, debating between a burger or the soggy tunafish sandwich his wife had made him. He would have probably decided on burgers by the time he had pushed through the door, the hefty bag of dead puppies barely clearing. He would have thrown the bag, like it was garbage, into his old red truck, then headed for the city dump.

Morgan hoped today she wouldn't run into the toothless dog catcher who was nice enough but always the bearer of new troubles and dogs that she didn't have time for or kennel space.

But, Morgan, even if she wanted to, couldn't ever turn down a dog that needed a home. Most often, when animals were brought to her, she would silently or openly chastise the dog-dumper, whether it was the dog's owner, a person who picked up the dog by chance, or even the dog catcher himself, who was only doing his job.

"One unwanted litter is born in the country every twenty seconds. There are not enough homes," she would cite at some point in the dog transfer despite there never being a good segue way. But Morgan really didn't care anymore. She had learned to like making dog-dumpers uncomfortable.

Because her right cheek was a little higher than her left, a forever reminder of a botched stitching job that Doc Jones, the local doctor, performed on her when she was only three and bitten by her mother's poodle, Tiny, Morgan, now fifty-five, looked as if she was smiling whether she was or not. This enigmatic quality almost always made the dog deliverer anxious when he or she heard Morgan quote the statistic while she was also smiling, sort of. Some felt guilty for bringing the dog to the shelter but most did not.

Morgan, a petite woman with down-turned eyes of steel-bright blue (like a Siberian husky or a catahoula dog, she liked to think), with a short, spiky gray hairdo, even had another scar, one on her lip, from yet another dog bite, causing the left side of her lip to curl when she spoke.

The cumulative effect of these flaws was that one couldn't tell if Morgan was happy, sad or mad, making most people uneasy about taking a dog to The Dog Lady as Morgan had become known. But Morgan's scars only heightened her beauty, casting it into a bas relief of sorts, encouraging people to hate her all the more. Some called her uppity until they needed a litter of pit bull mixes taken off their hands, Morgan not surprised by the sad fact that most of them were unwilling to waste their bullets killing the poor animals.

As Morgan hurried to the laundry room at the end of the hall, she glanced at the dogs as she passed the former bedrooms, two free-standing kennels in each. The dogs looked like four-legged specters, jumping and wailing, pleading to get out of the place. She quelled the urge to heave open the door and let them all go dog pile on the man with the rotting leg in the wheelchair, the old geezer rolling around in the parking lot when she drove in.

Morgan had a lot to do besides working all day at the dental office. Someone had called about a starving dog that had been on a chain for weeks. She needed to follow up on that. And since a volunteer had called in sick, she only had her lunch break to feed, water and clean up after twenty-five dogs, mop two-thousand square feet of cement floor, and wash and dry a couple of loads of dirty towels and blankets.

Her usual routine was dictated by strict parvovirus quarantine procedures, which lengthened the already arduous task.

Although parvo was a new disease to Morgan and the volunteers, it was common in most animal shelters. Puppies, because they hadn't been vaccinated, were usually the only ones who contracted it, but older dogs could get it too, especially if they hadn't had a parvo shot.

Remarkably, three puppies at the shelter with parvo had lived, succored back to health by one of their volunteers, Derril Harmon.

Abandoned on the side of a country road, the pups had been found by the toothless dog catcher, who had brought them to the shelter.

After Morgan injected them with Tamilflu, jump-starting their weak immune systems, Derril had taken them to his home in Fortville, Arkansas, twelve miles southeast of Multown, right across the Oklahoma border. For four days straight, he had force-fed them Pedialyte and baby cereal and injected them every two hours with potassium and dextrose. Derril had barely slept.

They became cute little poodly things adopted into poodly people homes. A modern-day miracle had occurred at McAfee Mutts. No one had ever heard of dogs surviving parvo, especially not in Oklahoma, where just about everything died young with or without a disease.

Among the volunteers, who ranged from retired school teachers to closet People for the Ethical Treatment of Animals (PETA) members to people who had adopted dogs from Morgan, Derril had become a bit of a legend. Not only was he fostering the maximum number of dogs allowed by a household in Fortville, which was six, but he had won McAfee Mutts Volunteer of the Year two years running.

The puppies she had euthanized last night had parvo. She made the hard choice to euthanize their mother as well. There was no room at the inn; besides, the mother would have grieved the loss of her babies.

As Morgan listened to the deafening din of the dogs howling and moaning in their kennels, her decision was confirmed: She could not handle any more homeless dogs today.

Since the kennels were in former bedrooms with no plumbing, volunteers filled jugs of water in the laundry room, where Ray had rigged up running water, then lugged the jug to the dogs. The farthest of the kennels was about fifty feet from the laundry room. Since no drainage system existed for the dogs' feces disposal, volunteers had to pick it up by hand, which made unpaid volunteers, already in short supply, even harder to come by. Thanks to Ray's dental practice, free latex gloves were abundant.

To make it even more difficult, teasing the volunteers like a shiny Dog Days Inn, was the new receiving-area-in-progress just outside the shelter, which Ray and Morgan had been working on since buying the nursing home a year ago.

They had custom-designed it with big, open kennels and a modern plumbing system featuring a connecting drain, where volunteers could hose out excrement. Morgan had another benefit planned in the fall to raise the sixty-thousand dollars left to finish the receiving center. But it was all they could do now to take care of and finance the homeless dogs they had. Her plans were off schedule, but, somehow, the dogs would have a better life than they had had so far.

Volunteers, for now, had to remove dog excrement the best way they could. The latest, all-in-one method, developed by Morgan, utilized a paint scraper to scoop the poop into a fireplace shovel with a sort of all-in-one motion, then, if that worked, dumping the waste into a lard bucket. This technique only worked on good poop days. Bad poop days were entirely a different story.

Morgan walked into the laundry room, threw one of Ray's old lab coats over her dress clothes, took off her pumps and pulled on muck boots, latex gloves and a face mask. She took fresh towels out of the dryer, put them in the wheeled laundry basket, then tossed a towel on the top of each kennel, out of the dogs' reach. After squirming through the kennel door and dancing through the jumping dogs, Morgan picked up a dirty towel that hopefully the dog had defecated upon, and placed it in the wheeled laundry basket in the hall.

Morgan had almost gathered all the soiled towels when she heard a high-pitched, humanlike scream. Running toward the noise, she dumped over the wheeled basket of dirty towels in the hallway. She prayed it wasn't another sick puppy, although it wouldn't have the strength to make any noise anyway. But it was only the black doberman, who had cornered a tiny black-and-white-spotted, semi-hairless dog with strange white wiry hair sprouting out of its head. The little dog was yelping at the top of its lungs.

"Oh, Dobber," Morgan scolded, pulling the big black dog away from the little one. "How did you get in here, you tiny thing? The pound guy must have put you here. I told him to put similar-sized dogs in the same kennels, not vice-versa."

Morgan rushed toward the kennel, almost forgetting to step in and out of the dish tub of bleach water sitting beside it, a parvo protocol. She pulled up the latch and stepped in, her wet boots slipping on the concrete floor. Morgan waved away the doberman and scooped up the little dog and turned it upright like a baby, its fringed paws pointing toward the exposed rafters, Ray removing the popcorn ceiling tiles to encourage more air circulation.

"Who are you, you spotted little clown? I see that you're a little girl," Morgan said, looking at the little dog's pink belly, bits of coarse white and black hair here and there. "And, of course, you're not fixed. I see no tattoo marking anyway."

Morgan pushed the little dog's hair out of her eyes and looked for a collar. "L-I-L-Y," Morgan said, reading the pink rhinestone letters out loud on the pretty blue collar. She fumbled around the dog's tiny neck for an identification tag but found none. Not even a microchip. "What a pretty collar. You must have belonged to someone special, Lily," Morgan said, petting the little dog. "But not special enough to tag you."

Morgan had only seen photos of Chinese-Cresteds, an exotic breed of dog she guessed to be Lily's pedigree, a pedigree made famous in America by entertainer Gypsy Rose Lee, she remembered. The little dog was, for the most part, hairless, with chocolate-colored spots sprinkled all over pinkish skin and long sprouts of coarse white hair on her feet, tail and head. She knew this was what was termed a hairless and there were long-haired versions called powderpuffs. "How could a human ever create something that looks like you?" Morgan tried to run her fingers through Lily's topknot, but the little dog's hair was too matted and dirty. "You look like you have a comb-over. Humans are sick creatures."

Morgan tried to push the big black dog off her when its front paws latched around her legs. "Get down, Dobie. Shelter dogs and their attachment issues." She tried doing the same with Lily, the little dog stuck tight around her neck like a furry boa constrictor, but she wouldn't budge either.

Morgan finally pried off the doberman but gave up doing the same with Lily. She carried the little dog into the next kennel, where Buddy, who had been at McAfee Mutts as long as Morgan could remember, jumped up, eyeing his new visitor. The one-eyed, once-snow white schnauzer had been in and out of foster homes for so many years that he had turned a light gray. She tried to put Lily down again, but nothing was about to make the dog let go of Morgan now.

While Lily's claws were embedded in Morgan's lab coat, Morgan, with gloved hands, picked up the excrement then carefully placed it into a Walmart bag, tossing it into a wheeled trashcan in the hallway between the rooms.

The mopping was next. Volunteers were instructed to mix five ounces of bleach per gallon of water and to change and remake that solution after every kennel was mopped, cleaning each kennel with a fresh batch of bleach solution. If the mixture was too strong, the dogs, especially light-colored ones, could have allergic reactions. If the mixture was too weak, it wouldn't deter the parvo.

Morgan mixed the solution with Lily riveted to her hip and mopped while Lily sat in the squeegee bucket. Lily taunted the other dogs by yipping from the other side of the kennel while the other dogs, taking her bait, jumped up and down, barking wildly.

Next, Morgan fed the dogs ample helpings of donated dog food, both wet and dry, topped with bright-colored treats made like Christmas trees and stars. A baker from eastern Arkansas had donated three-thousand pounds of these special treats, which were so heavy that Ray's truck scraped the highway on the way back to Multown. Morgan always wanted the dogs to have a full tummy, especially since they might possibly be having their last supper, although Morgan euthanized as few dogs as possible and tried to find homes for as many as she could.

Tonight, in order to make Lily her own, Morgan would have to do a little extra something for Ray. She would put all of her house dogs that slept in their bed with them into the bathroom and close the door. She would try to ignore the dogs' yelps while she and Ray made love in the bedroom. Ray, because he was always so exhausted, might not even notice the addition of one more house dog to the ever-growing dog posse that belonged to Morgan, which, at last count, was up to seven. And if things went well tonight, with the addition of Lily, would become eight.

In her seven years since chartering McAfee's Mutts as a charity in addition to assuming responsibility for the Multown pound, Morgan had found homes for more than two thousand dogs. The seventy-five or so dogs (she didn't know the number exactly because she had lost count) that had not been euthanized or adopted lived at her house in their three-acre backyard.

Fosters took care of approximately thirty-five more dogs.

And the numbers were growing. Forty years ago, what had started as one dog, a little border collie named Sheba and then one more dog, Charlie, a rescue from Fortville's animal shelter, where Morgan had volunteered for five years and formerly served on its board, now totaled more than one hundred animals available for adoption.

When she was sixteen, Morgan had rescued Sheba after the dog had been hit by a car in the middle of Highway 64. Cars whizzed by the convulsing animal until Morgan stopped traffic to get the dog and rushed her to the vet. Sheba had lived for many years with Morgan and Ray until the beloved dog's death.

Her next rescue dog, Charlie, was an impounded Rottweiler that Morgan had demanded to see when he was locked behind the no-public-allowed doors at the Fortville Animal Shelter. She had rescued Charlie from a dismal cell containing a single bowl of dirty water.

Despite raising two children, working full time and ignoring Ray's pleas to quit taking dogs,

Morgan never stopped, believing the dogs deserved not only a life but a damned good life. Ray had finally given up since Ray loved Morgan as much as Morgan loved dogs.

    Lily was still attached to Morgan's shirt when she pulled the old Chevy van donated by her rich brother-in-law into the dental office five minutes late. In her head, she could hear Nelda, the crotchety dental assistant, complaining about the phones that had gone unanswered in Morgan's absence since Morgan was also the receptionist in addition to office manager.

    Morgan peeled Lily from her, placed her in the passenger seat of the van and poured water into a collapsible bowl. She cracked the windows, stepped out of the car and shut the door. "Now you be quiet," Morgan said, shaking a finger at the little dog looking pitifully at her through the dirty van window. "I've got to get Ray prepared for you."

    But Lily wouldn't quit whining. Morgan yanked open the van door, grabbed up Lily and tucked the noisy, nearly naked little dog into her purse. "Now, hush, or I'm not taking you in," said Morgan, looking crazy, talking to her purse, Lily not visible.

While Lily sat under Morgan's desk in her lap the rest of the day, Morgan checked in and out dental patients and answered the phone. Nobody seemed to notice Morgan's grimaces, Lily's claws embedded in the crotch of Morgan's pants.

Beatrice-Chapter Three

Martina's last litter was about to be born.

Beatrice was so excited she had planned a birthing day party for Martina the day before the little dog was to go into labor, which had always been on time. The Italian greyhound never had any trouble during any of her previous fourteen deliveries. Martina was perfect. Beatrice anticipated no problems.

Beatrice's friends had all come, including Dotty, who bought Martina the cutest Babies on Board t-shirt, which Martina had worn and was tight on her, the usually svelte canine's teats now engorged with milk.

Beatrice and her friends had gathered around the kitchen table, Martina wearing a little party hat made by Dotty and sitting like a child in a highchair, a little strap around her belly bump holding her in place. Her forepaws, bedecked with bright pink toenails, rested on the tray.

Beatrice had bought the most expensive champagne she could find and poured it into glasses mail-ordered from a fancy department store.

"To Martina," Beatrice had said, being careful not to break the delicate crystal in her bearlike paw of a hand and motioning the glass toward Martina. "May this be the best litter of puppies ever."

Martina was the color of silver in the sunset. She was a show dog, famous in Arkansas, Oklahoma and Missouri, for birthing the most mini of Italian greyhounds, a breed already small to begin with. Martina's offspring had even more delicate bones than normal with limbs that looked as if the slightest wind might break them. Martina was also well known for winning blue ribbons twice her size. And it didn't hurt the little greyhound's success that raising dogs was in Beatrice's genes.

Beatrice's mother, a large woman named Berta, a long-time breeder of Bernese mountain dogs who also ran the manufacturing line at the air conditioner plant in Fortville, had wanted Beatrice to breed sturdy working dogs with meat on their bones. Berta, a woman who prided herself on pragmatism, had urged her daughter to produce useful dogs capable of surviving the area's roller-coaster weather that zig-zagged from frigid winters to stifling summers.

Fortville, where Beatrice and Martina made their home, was originally a rough and tough border town that straddled eastern Oklahoma and western Arkansas. Developed in the early eighteen-hundreds to keep the warring Indian tribes apart and law in Indian Territory (now Oklahoma), the town had since lost much of its testosterone. And even though it had been dumbed down into a boring manufacturing city, Fortville was still not the safest place for miniature Italian greyhounds nor their gay owners. But Beatrice, despite the odds and one-sixteenth Cherokee blood herself, had fallen in love with Italian greyhounds after seeing her idol, a host of a home-improvement show, with one of the fine-boned animals perched atop his lap during a television interview.

Beatrice had traveled all the way to New York City to get an Italian greyhound puppy, the breeder claiming it to be a relative of the reality show star's dog. But after Beatrice cupped baby Martina in one of her huge hands, she couldn't care less about Martina's family tree.

Beatrice tried hard not to give a damn what her mother would think, although Beatrice worshipped her mother. Beatrice attempted to hide Martina from Big Berta, but when her mother came to visit and almost crushed Martina under one of her steel-toed boots, the gig was up. Beatrice, scared for Martina's life and her own, had whisked Martina up in her arms, espousing her helpless devotion for the delicate animal, while Berta loudly questioned the American Dog Club's judgment in registering vermin.

Beatrice, a big-boned woman like her mother, was very self-conscious about her size. So Beatrice had reasoned that Martina, by association, might make her look smaller, but the Italian greyhound had the opposite effect: Beatrice looked even bigger when she and Martina were together.

Hoping that more dogs might make her size less noticeable, she added Bay-Bay and Rihanna, two females from Martina's first litter born seven years ago.

Every evening, after working at Computerville, Beatrice would exercise "the girls," walking the three greyhounds on her quaint neighborhood's brick sidewalks that lined the post-World War II houses with their Victory chimneys, so named for a "V" masoned in the brick.

The greyhounds would prance, like miniature Lipizzan stallions, in a straight line precisely two feet in front of Beatrice's Birkenstock sandals, Beatrice wearing one of her seven pairs of black jeans and one of her seven black t-shirts. In the winter months, she wore black turtlenecks and black socks. Beatrice, who aimed to be more practical like her mother and prided herself on her streamlined utilitarianism, had only one extravagance: The dogs had more clothes than Beatrice.

Beatrice, a shy computer programmer who had just turned 35, would also use the greyhounds as a conversation piece, giving her twelve skinny legs of social lubricant for neighborly confabs.

She had even met her lover, Dotty, during one of her neighborhood walks with her dogs. Blonde and skinny Dotty, who was endowed with a bounciness that irritated most, lived in the same historic area as Beatrice and, coincidentally, owned a male Italian greyhound, Pesto. Beatrice accused Dotty of stalking her and buying the dog just to make her acquaintance but was flattered just the same.

Dotty, who was also patriotic to the point of owning an American-flag-emblazoned brassier, had even convinced Beatrice to join a city-commissioned animal committee that was currently reviewing Fortville's animal laws. "We can celebrate our mutual love of dogs and give a little back to a city and country that has been so good to us," Dotty had said while bouncing Pesto on her lap during a fireworks display. Regretfully afterward, Pesto, all decked out in an Uncle Sam outfit, had tossed up his blue doggy treats all over Dotty.

As part of this animal committee, Beatrice and Dotty had worked together many late nights preparing a report that refuted a recent city ordinance proposal that would license dog breeders as well as require dog owners to spay or neuter their dogs. Beatrice thought it was a far cry from fixing the problem of a loose dog running around to passing a spay/neuter mandate for all dogs. She was going to do everything she could to make sure it didn't pass.

Beatrice affectionately called her greyhounds her "skinny bitches," outfitting them in sweaters and matching booties year-round. But even in the summers, the greyhounds, draped in their heavy sweaters, would shiver because they were so damned skinny.

Beatrice had texted all her breeder friends when, right on schedule, Martina had laid her bony little body down in the special birthing bed with its detachable, washable cover that Beatrice had ordered from her favorite online pet boutique. But, Martina, being the perfect dog, never bore babies with much afterbirth. She aimed to please her master, who didn't like messes either.

Martina brought a fine price for her puppies. She had won many prizes in dog shows, almost fetching Best in Show last year in Tulsa. Beatrice hated to retire her but knew she had to because Martina, now eight, was getting too old and each labor was putting her at risk. This would be her last litter.

She had hoped Bay-Bay and Rihanna would follow in Martina's paw prints, but Bay-Bay had a nervous condition that caused her to defecate on the judges when they would look under her tail. And Rihanna had a doggy Turret's Syndrome that manifested in the dog running in circles and yipping at the top of her little lungs when being shown.

So Beatrice hoped for a good dog from this litter. One that would win prizes again. However, this was Pesto's first litter. Beatrice had wanted a much more seasoned sire, but Dotty had begged Beatrice for the opportunity to let her little man take the helm. Beatrice had regretted the decision six hours into Pesto and Martina's hook-up as the two skinny dogs glared at one another down their fine-boned noses instead of doing the job that nature intended.

Dotty had thought a little pate dabbed on Martina's private parts might incentivize the love-making, but it only encouraged Martina to lick herself inappropriately. Beatrice had muzzled her, which was probably a good idea anyway. Pesto had finally mounted Martina, unsure of what to do once he got there, Pesto not one for heights. The awkward ordeal, resembling two matchsticks rubbing up on one another with a few squeaky, pitiful moans thrown in, had only lasted a few moments. In celebration, Beatrice and Dotty had lit cigarettes afterward, although being non-smokers, they quickly snuffed them out in the sink and sprayed the room with air freshener.

Now, exactly six months later, it was showtime as Martina circled the bed's interior, trying to find the best spot to lie down.

Beatrice had boiled water and readied thick towels, a routine she thought gave her luck but, more or less, just calmed her down a little. Beatrice, normally laid back, was a bit high strung on these occasions. She had set the thermostat up to eighty and placed Martina's bed in the first rays of the gloaming spilling through the western window of the girls' bedroom. Martina kneaded her delicate little paws into the memory foam of her custom pet bed several hundred times and finally settled on a spot to lie down. She rolled onto her side and grunted, uncommon for the stoic greyhound. Beatrice kneeled beside the bed and stroked the shivering and shaking Martina, Beatrice pulling a blanket over her.

Craning her neck up and out, Martina's four limp legs stuck out to the side of her pregnant belly, Martina tried to make eye contact with Beatrice but couldn't, so Beatrice held up the little dog's delicate head so they could see one another. "Come on, my girl," Beatrice said, urging the little dog on. "This is the last litter, I promise."

Beatrice stared at herself reflected back in the little black pools of liquid devotion until she disappeared. Martina even died perfectly.

No muss, no fuss.

Lily-Chapter 4

Lily was free. Out of the prison. Away from The Big Black Dog that wouldn't leave her alone.

She had spent her first night with The Lady with Sad Eyes who lived in the biggest doghouse ever with seven other dogs. Now, the morning after, Lily was outside of what she hoped was her new forever home, trying to outrun the hot breeze as fast as her little legs would carry her.

Lily stopped and shook like a tiny horizontal tornado, the dew flying from her, what few tufts of hair she had bristled up toward the sky. The neat little dog couldn't stand her hair mussed or even wet. She had been so filthy when The Man with the Hole in His Smile had scooped her up, thrown her into a metal box and taken her to that hell from which she had just escaped. Her fine coat had been a continuous black smudge, her fair skin sunburnt.

But last night, The Lady with Sad Eyes had given Lily a bath in a tub while, much to Lily's dismay, seven other dogs watched. She had her pride.

Now a squeaky-clean Lily was running fast and free outside again, although there were more dogs than Lily had ever seen: big ones, furry ones, cute ones, unfriendly ones, nervous ones, little ones and really ugly ones. They were all, thank goodness, in pens that were bigger than those in that dark dungeon, but they were in pens, nonetheless. Here there were both inside and outside dogs.

She had tried to say hello to some but not to all of them, especially the ones that growled, but Lily didn't care. She was free again. She might have a nasty attitude, too, if she was still in prison. Maybe she would come back later and try to make friends. But not now. She had better things to do, like playing in the grass, running faster and faster, making herself dizzy.

Then, all at once, the sun disappeared, catapulting Lily's world from light to dark. The frightened dog planted her tufted paws into the grass, screeching her little body to a halt, the dog tumbling end over end. She lay in the grass, wondering what had just happened until, finally, she opened her eyes and blinked. It was still dark, but Lily could see.

Four of the longest legs ever, shiny black paws at their ends, surrounded her. A big belly with a funny spout hovered above. Lily heard a sniffly bark coming from the opposite end of the spout and tried to gather the courage to figure out where it was coming from. She craned her neck out only to discover a sky of grass beyond the two longest legs ever, nothing more.

When she heard the bark again, Lily rolled over and scurried to her tufted paws. Frozen, she stared again at the legs that looked even longer, right side up. Lily felt a warm spray on her fine head and glanced up to a terrible stinging sensation. Blinded,

Lily ran as fast as she could until she felt the warm sun once again.

Lily took a few deep breaths and opened her eyes and blinked until her vision cleared. Standing before her was The Biggest Dog Ever, a *spotted one,* just like Lily. Lily turned and ran as hard as she could back in what she hoped was the same direction. She ran and ran until she couldn't run anymore. Exhausted, she glanced behind her to see if the big dog was after her. It wasn't. But Lily kept her eyes open just in case.

Lily had never felt so alive and free. Not even when The Man with Kind Eyes would beg Lily to sit and lie down or count, especially when others, like The Lady with Mean Eyes, was around to watch. He also liked to give treats when the little dog would do her tricks, which was okay with Lily, though it wasn't that much trouble to do the stuff they wanted. There were treats here, too, only most were broken or a little stale but just as good. The Lady with Sad Eyes would give them to Lily for no reason at all. Lily didn't have to do a thing.

Lily thought her brother Fredo would like it here. He was always getting into trouble where they had lived. Maybe he could come visit her sometime soon. He liked to go visiting, but The Man with Kind Eyes hadn't liked that and was always leaving in one of those Big Noisy Things to retrieve Fredo.

Lily had spent most of last night safely tucked inside a furry ball of dogness, all her new friends lying next to a tall water bowl that The Lady with Sad Eyes or The Man with Old Eyes would sit on or stand beside and put their water into.

But last night hadn't started out so cozy.

Most of the inside dogs had ganged up on Lily when The Lady with Sad Eyes was gone. But a brown inside dog with a white bib on his puffed chest had taken up for Lily, snarling the other dogs away. The other dogs, after feeling sorry for themselves, had come back and lay with Lily and her new friend, who let Lily tuck herself between his paws.

"You will come to bed with us tomorrow night," The Lady with Sad Eyes had said last night while sitting atop the tall water bowl and reaching down to scratch Lily's ears, Lily resting between The Lady with Sad Eyes' furry feet.

The Lady with Sad Eyes had pulled down on the tail of the tall water bowl, which, though it had concerned Lily, hadn't stopped the little dog from wanting to sleep with The Lady with Sad Eyes. But Lily hoped she wouldn't pull her tail. Lily loved her little pouf at the tip and didn't want to lose it.

Lily threw herself on the grass, exhausted, The Biggest Dog Ever seemingly at bay, when The Curly-Haired Dog, the one with the silly bows in its ears, one of the troublemakers from last night, jumped on her.

Lily bit his ear before she could stop herself, sending The Curly-Haired Dog speeding in the direction of the big doghouse where they had both spent last night together.

The little dog thought she might take the other silly bow out later. But Lily, not one to second-guess herself, wasn't sure if that would be wise. She decided to go find The Lady with Sad Eyes. She would know what to do.

Morgan-Chapter 5

Morning came early at the McAfee house, a big split-level cedar and rock house out in the country, three miles west of Multown. Ray and Morgan had built it right after they were married in 1979, when they were still a little bit hippy, before kids, life and dogs took over.

Morgan's mother lived on an adjoining fifty acres to the west in a small, plain white wood-frame house that Morgan had grown up in. Morgan had never veered too far from her home, not even leaving for college. And though Morgan secretly wished she had seen more of the world, she hadn't taken to what she had seen so far, imagining the world beyond her neck of the woods not much better.

The McAfees lived on fifty acres, almost every square foot of it teeming with some sort of living creature, whether it was dog, cat, horse or hamster. Mortimer, the white hamster, a pet of Morgan's two grown children, both grown with one in vet school, had been accidentally let out of his cage ten years ago. So Mortimer, after slipping through the sliding glass door, had been living on his own, outside in the elements. No one really worried about him because he was a resourceful hamster, spending his winters in the barn and the other three seasons in the fields, not too far from the dog runs. If he was quick enough to outmaneuver the other critters, he could eat the leftover cat and dog food, which kept him in fine form for a hamster, especially an elderly one.

At five o'clock every morning, Ray and Morgan rolled out of bed and pulled on their coveralls lying on the floor, the outside dogs' hungry cries a relentless alarm clock. The inside dogs, the ones that weren't already licking the McAfees' faces, aroused from their doggy dreams.

Morning feedings ran about an hour depending on how many dogs the McAfees were fostering, an exact figure never known, there never enough time to figure it.

But when pressed by other visitors to the animal menagerie, Morgan would mumble "probably seventy-five dogs, three horses and twenty-plus cats, give or take a few." It sounded so absurd when she said it out loud that she didn't like to say it out loud. Most of the medicine, ranging from topical creams to heart worm pills to flea treatment to shots, was also administered in the morning, making the morning routine a hullabaloo but a well-orchestrated one.

The seventy-five or so dogs, depending on their temperament, behavior and size, lived outside at the McAfee house in six separate, fenced-in areas with each dog getting his very own doghouse. An air-conditioned feed room housed several of the elderly dogs and luckier cats, who hung out in a glass aviary that Ray transformed into what he jokingly called his glass cat house.

In the barn, Morgan and Ray were feeding Daisy, an appaloosa Morgan had rescued several years ago. The cats, which hadn't been fed yet, were pacing along the edge of the loft, some of them stopping to swipe the air with a paw, looking for attention.

Morgan, trying to recall the jutting ridges of hip bones that once loomed above a barren valley of what was formerly a horse's back, petted the now-lovely Daisy on her dappled, velvet nose, holding the feed bucket up to her mouth so the horse could get every drop.

Morgan had been trying to adopt Daisy for three years on the shelter's website but hadn't had a bite. A horse's upkeep was expensive, cumbersome and time consuming; adopters were rare. One volunteer had rescued another horse and recently adopted her, proving it could be done with tremendous effort and luck.

The Tulsa newspaper had reported that people who owned horses didn't have much money nowadays to keep one up, attributing it to a bad state and national economy, so horses paid the price. In Oklahoma, one could drive for only a few miles before seeing a starving horse in a pasture. People had been selling horses illegally to meat processing plants, which distributed the meat to other countries. The Oklahoma Legislature had just passed a law allowing horses to be slaughtered again after being outlawed for fifty years. Legislators said so many horses were starving anyway, so why not kill them, make a little money and feed somebody.

Morgan couldn't imagine eating a cow, let alone a horse for she had grown up on one. One of her few memories of her father, long gone, was of him stumbling around, two six packs of Busch beer in him, leading Morgan around on her old horse, Blaze, a rag rug for a saddle.

To the east, the big fiery orange ball crept over the spindly river oaks' bony fingers, reminding the McAfees that the day had begun and time was running out to get to their world of people, good and bad, with teeth, good and bad. The illegal methamphetamine drug epidemic had rendered a good part of Multown's population with blackened, decayed teeth. Meth mouth it was called. This sometimes meant a little more business for Ray but only if the meth-heads had Medicaid. Ray's practice kept the dogs in food, treats, medicine and vet care. The Fortville dog plant donated some dog food but not nearly enough. Private donations helped foot much of the bill.

Lily, barking, ran up to Morgan and Ray.

"Hush, Lily. You'll scare Daisy," Morgan said, surprised to see the little dog so far from the house.

Scampering out of his reach, Lily continued barking as Ray tried to grab her. "Lily, come here, now," Ray yelled. "Morgan, please get her out of here. I've got to get this done and get to work. You do, too."

Morgan was smiling, secretly admiring Lily's bravado. She finished putting the sweet feed in the trough, folded the sack, tucked it under her arm and watched Ray and Lily go after each other. Lily shimmied out of his reach in an ever-widening perimeter. "Morgan," Ray said, grabbing for Lily again and missing, Ray almost falling. "You've got to get that dog out of here. Daisy could kick her."

Morgan walked toward Lily then stopped and patted the top of her thigh. "Come, Lily."

Morgan bent over and Lily jumped into her arms as the empty sack of sweet feed fell out from under Morgan's arm.

Ray grabbed the empty sack and headed back to the feed room, his bald head a pinky-orange shade silhouetted in the sunrise. He nodded to the dry ground. "She's trouble. I know it."

Morgan kissed the little dog on her pointed, speckled nose and brushed the blades of grass from her crested head. "What am I going to do with you? You are such a princess. And a wet one at that." Morgan sniffed Lily. "And stinky already. Geez, I just washed you last night in the bathtub. You smell like horse urine."

Daisy whinnied in their direction. Morgan, with Lily in hand, planned on making an introduction between the two when Daisy curled back her black lips and nipped at the little dog. Morgan brushed the horse away and tucked Lily close. "Stop it, Daisy. What's up with this bad behavior? Have you guys met before? It seems like you have."

Lily nipped back at the horse, just barely missing Morgan's bare hand. "Yes, you have met before, I see. You've made a lot of friends, Lily. Miss Congeniality on the first day here at my house."

While Ray fed the other two horses, the shetland, Prissy, and a black gelding, Lost (so named because he had been found running along a busy road in Fortville and no one would claim him), Morgan took Lily inside. She put Lily down in the floor of the living room with the other house dogs and headed back out the door to finish the morning rounds. Morgan heard Lily growl and reeled around, just grabbing her before the little dog nipped Alfonse, the old white poodle. Morgan saw that one of his bows was missing from his ears and bent down to look closer. She spied a tiny bite mark on the old poodle's left ear, a bite mark that could only belong to Lily.

"Shame on you, Lily, for biting poor Alfonse."

But Lily only wagged her tail in response.

Morgan checked the clock. It was ten till eight o'clock. She had to be to work, and it took ten minutes to drive into Multown. She was running late. What was she going to do with Lily while she finished feeding the dogs? She didn't want to leave her alone just yet.

Remembering an old baby carrier she had used for her kids, Morgan rushed up the stairs. She pulled it out of the hall closet, dusted it off, tied it around her and ran back down the stairs. Morgan scooped up Lily, plopped her in the carrier, and went out to finish the morning rounds. Morgan didn't like to show favoritism, but Lily, such a diva, demanded attention.

When Jake the bulldog almost bit Lily, Morgan turned the baby carrier around, putting Lily in the small of her back so Lily would have a more difficult time antagonizing the dogs. Vocalizing her dismay, Lily whined the rest of the time.

After Morgan finished feeding the dogs, she ran back into the house, ripped off the baby carrier and dumped Lily on the couch. Morgan charged up the stairs and ran into her bedroom, this time changing from her coveralls into a dress of her mother's she had recently found in her mother's closet. Morgan didn't feel right buying new clothes for herself with all the money the McAfees spent on dogs, so she would only allow herself thrift shop purchases or hand-me-downs from her daughter in vet school. She slipped on the store-bought purple cotton A-line skirt and matching blazer, which was in pristine condition though probably purchased almost five decades ago. Morgan supposed it must have been one of her mother's church dresses because Morgan, for the life of her, couldn't remember it. Morgan never attended church with her mother, not even when Morgan was little. Morgan had preferred spending that time in the old pecan tree with her cats. She was a self-proclaimed atheist but lately had called on God to help her. Though it was hypocritical, Morgan didn't feel an ounce of guilt, feeling justified in asking for all the help she could get.

Finally, Morgan jumped into her old Mercedes and headed for the office. She backed out of the driveway, checking for random dogs behind her. Sometimes, dogs got loose despite all the precautions to keep them safe in a secure area.

Her cell phone rang, which was unusual. She didn't give out her cell phone number because five to six animal calls were already coming in daily to the office and her home from local law enforcement since there was no humane society in Summerland County. If she gave out her cell phone number, she would have none of her life left and could get nothing done. She expected it was Ray.

Morgan flipped open the phone, almost tossing it over her head. She jammed it to her ear. "I just headed out. I'll be there in ten minutes," Morgan said. She waited for a response from Ray but heard an unfamiliar clearing of the throat instead.

"Morgan, hey, I'm sorry. This is Derril Harmon." Derril was Morgan's best volunteer and a perennial bachelor who, at age fifty-six, still lived with his mother in Fortville. "I need some help. I'm not sure what else to do." He paused for a moment, waiting for a reply from Morgan. She hoped one of the foster dogs that Derril had taken from her wasn't sick. "It's about this city ordinance that we're trying to get passed here in Fortville that would require people to get their dog fixed."

He paused again. Morgan said nothing but sighed with relief thinking the foster dogs were apparently okay.

"Morgan?" Derril asked, wondering if she was still on the line.

"Yes?" Morgan answered, waiting for one of her many adoptable cats to cross the driveway so she could drive to the gate.

"I think it would help with the animal overpopulation over here in Fortville," Derril continued, Morgan trying her best to concentrate on what he was saying. "I think if dogs had to be fixed, there would be fewer animals running the streets and ending up at the shelter and then euthanized cause there aren't enough homes."

Morgan had heard about these new spay/neuter laws from one of her friends who performed spay/neuters for many low-income areas in Oklahoma and its Indian reservations. She knew Tulsa and Lawton and North Little Rock had passed these ordinances. She was interested. Since so many people from Fortville called her for assistance with homeless animals, Morgan felt she had a stake in their animal welfare laws.

"Last week, it passed the first vote four to three, but they say one of the those directors that passed it the first time may be changing his mind for the second reading. And, if that director votes against it, it'll be four against three, and then there will be one more reading. It has to be read three times if it doesn't receive at least five votes one way or another. And if it fails again, its dead. We need to drum up support for it or it will die. I'm at an impasse. The animal committee commissioned to investigate its effectiveness is also presenting their findings tonight." He paused for just a moment. "And they're against it too, I heard."

Morgan liked Derril, but what on earth could she do about politics? She didn't have the time. But she liked Derril and, after all, he had done so much for the shelter. Cradling her old flip-phone to her ear, Morgan got out of the car and opened the heavy iron gate that corralled the animals in case they got out of their fenced-in areas.

"Hey, Derril, I don't know about that. How could I help you?"

Morgan heard a crash and looked up just in time to see an old yellow Datsun plummeting through the McAfee's chain link fence. Next, a river of dogs was pouring out of a gaping hole and flowing into a ditch. Past that ditch was Highway 64, cars whizzing by on their way to work. Morgan heard a long tire screech and held her breath, praying that no thud would follow.

"Derril, I'm sorry, I gotta go. I'll call you later." Morgan wished she had treats in the pockets of her mother's dress instead of mothballs. She threw down the phone, pushed open the gate and ran toward the gushing dog river.

Beatrice-Chapter 6

    Beatrice didn't like a busy four-lane highway so close to Martina's gravesite. The little greyhound had been afraid of cars. Martina would be able to hear the hundreds of homeless mutts barking frantically, their mournful howls and moans like sick, sad poison seeping through the cement-bricked walls of the Fortville Animal Shelter. It wasn't where Beatrice preferred to bury Martina, but, for the life of her, she couldn't think of anywhere else.

    Beatrice, dressed in her black-on-black jeans and t-shirt ensemble, pitched her large cranium back on her thick neck, her short red hair tickling the back of it. She gazed at the blue sky as a white puffy cumulus cloud, seemingly unfazed by the shitty world it presided over, ambled along, the crispy leaves of several large pin oak trees framing Beatrice's view. Beatrice tried to remember if Martina had looked up that much to even know that a sky existed and could barely remember Martina even looking at her, except when Martina was dying. Martina had been so demure. Surely she liked trees. All dogs liked trees. Beatrice hoped the little greyhound would like it here.

Martina's funeral was well attended by several of Beatrice and Dotty's friends, plus Bay-Bay, Rihanna and Pesto. Even the president of the Tulsa chapter of the American Dog Club, along with his standard schnauzers, Adolf and Eva, in their matching Scottish Fair Isle sweaters in spite of it being the hottest day of the year, had come to pay their condolences.

Beatrice finally agreed to buy Martina a burial plot at the Fortville Pet Cemetery but only with much prodding from Dotty, who was on the Fortville Humane Society's board of directors, the non-profit also the cemetery's caretaker. The Fortville Humane Society also ran the Fortville Animal Shelter. All three entities were located in the same block on the city's north side, the opposite side of the town where Beatrice and Dotty lived.

At first, Beatrice was dead set against burying Martina so far away from home, but Beatrice knew if she buried Martina in her own backyard, she couldn't bear it. Thus Beatrice had conceded to Dotty's wishes. "But I do not like that she's spending eternity next to a mutt. She will have mutts running all over her grave," Beatrice had said to Dotty after handing a check to the cashier, whom Beatrice thought looked like a mutt himself, all tattoos and greasy green hair, slumping behind the Fortville Humane Society counter. Beatrice and Dotty had purchased the plot during their lunch hours the day after Martina's passing.

"You'll be happy to know she'll be buried next to a purebred Yorkie," Dotty had said, patting Beatrice on her big back consolingly. "I made sure of it. And there won't be mutts running over it unless the shelter dogs are walked, which doesn't happen that often. They're supposed to walk the shelter dogs *around* the graveyard anyway." Dotty shook her head, looking down at the counter. "I mean, the *those-that-have-passed* yard."

But during Martina's funeral service, as Beatrice recited Martina's homage that Beatrice had written on her computer tablet, the screen smudged from her big tears, Beatrice happened to notice the headstone on the grave next to Martina's plot said, *Here Lies the Terminator* and screeched her eulogy to a halt.

"I thought you said it was a *Yorkie,*" said Beatrice, turning and grabbing Dotty, Pesto, Bay-Bay and Rihanna on leashes in Dotty's hand.

Dotty managed to squirm out of Beatrice's large grasp. "It *is* a Yorkie," Dotty tried to explain, hand-ironing the sleeve of her lacy white-cotton dress. "It *could* be a *Yorkie* named *Terminator,*" she said as Beatrice tried to grab Dotty again but Dotty dancing out of her reach. "It could be," Dotty pleaded.

Bay-Bay and Pesto whined while Rihanna chased her tail, winding the three leashes round and round herself and the other Italian greyhounds. It would only be a few seconds before Bay-Bay would take a dump.

But Beatrice was ready to bury Martina; it had been four days since the greyhound's death, after all. So Beatrice motioned, with her big hand, for the shelter worker to put Martina's steel casket into the eighteen-inch-deep hole that Beatrice had specified for Martina's internment, a depth she had found on the Internet as best for keeping critters at bay.

Beatrice had already said her good-byes to Martina anyway. She had slept with Martina in her bed last night, and though the little dog's body was stiff after embalming, Beatrice cried like a baby and managed to fashion Martina into a semblance of a fetal position, spooning the rigid Martina.

Beatrice had kissed Martina on her tiny, tight forehead that morning and placed her atop the creamy, pearl-colored satin bedding of the casket. She had put Martina on her side and positioned the little greyhound's forepaws one over the other because Martina was and would always be, even in her death, a lady. Beatrice had left around the little dog's neck the blue leather collar with pink rhinestones.

Beatrice watched as the shelter worker tripped and tossed Martina's tiny casket into the thick

August air. She hoped the casket wouldn't hit the hard ground and burst open to catapult out poor dead Martina. But the chances of that weren't looking too good.

That evening, after Martina's funeral and all the guests had gone, Beatrice had only an hour to finish the report on the findings of the city's animal committee that she and Dotty had headed. The meeting was that night, so she had set up her laptop in the coffee shop where there would be no distractions.

Beatrice was excited because she had found information that would bury Fortville City Councilman Lance Blackmon and his stupid spay/neuter ordinance once and for all, Beatrice planning to bury both in a very shallow grave so, in fact, the critters *could* get them. As Beatrice keyed in the thirteen animal care and control recommendations, her big fingers fumbled on the inchoate keyboard of her computer tablet. She licked her lips, anticipating the night's political victory.

Beatrice had recently taken an active role in city government and graduated valedictorian of her citizens' academy class. She wanted to be mayor someday, but, more importantly, she wanted to set a good example for other gays in Fortville. But before any kind of political run, Beatrice would need to pay her civic dues, which she was doing. She wasn't sure if Fortville was ready for a gay mayor. Or even a female mayor, for that matter.

    Beatrice took a sip of her iced cinnamon cafe latte and smiled a very big smile, which was unusual because Beatrice had had bad teeth and hardly ever smiled. Though her mother had kept her precious Bernese mountain dogs' teeth clean and brushed them every night, she had neglected to instill good dental hygiene practices into Beatrice and her twin brother, Ben. As a result of this maternal oversight, Beatrice had had to have all her teeth removed and replaced with dental implants. She was still self conscious, even though her ivories gleamed now as white as Chiclets. But when Beatrice smiled, she still pursed her lips tight and scrunched up her nose like she had eaten a green persimmon, old habits dying hard. But not tonight for she would smile openly.

Councilman Lance Blackmon wouldn't smile though. When he read Beatrice's report at City Council tonight, he would squirm as his left eye blinked on and off again, the effect magnified under those thick black glasses. Blackmon would resemble a goggly-eyed lighthouse, although Beatrice had never seen an actual lighthouse, either plain or goggly-eyed. Beatrice's animal committee had found Blackmon's proposed spay/neuter ordinance lacked balls, so to speak. Two weeks ago, after the proposed spay/neuter ordinance had passed on its first vote by four of the seven city councilman, one of the councilmen, Gary Rhodes, who had voted against it, commissioned Beatrice's animal committee to further investigate the effectiveness of the spay/neuter law. Beatrice had met Gary at the citizens academy class where Beatrice had taken Gary's class on Robert's Rules of Order. And Gary, familiar with Beatrice's love of dogs, had asked her to head the animal committee. Beatrice had been honored.

But since the proposed ordinance's first vote reading didn't get approved by at least five councilmen, two more consecutive readings would be required to determine the ordinance's final outcome. If Beatrice had her way, it would be voted down that night, seven to zip, which could only happen if the three-reading rule were suspended, which required a five-vote majority to overrule it.

Beatrice thought of Martina alone in that graveyard, surrounded by mutts, both dead and still living, until her thoughts swerved, much to her dismay, to Anne Meyers: the perfectly pedigreed Anne Meyers who always wore designer, the Anne Meyers who, of course, was homecoming queen, the Anne Meyers who was valedictorian, thus relegating Beatrice to the sad salutatorian spot.

Meyers was the sole city councilwoman on the Fortville City Council who always voted in lockstep with Blackmon. Her father, Billy Bob Sterling, the patriarch of double-wide trailer sales, was also, somewhat surprisingly, an animal welfare leader and ran the low-cost spay/neuter veterinary clinic in town. Sterling, who was already filthy rich, would make even more money when people had to get their dogs fixed and probably sell more double-wide trailers as a result. It was such a coup. Beatrice was having none of it.

Mandatory pet registration, another idea authored by Blackmon as part of his silly spay/neuter ordinance, was also just plain stupid. Nobody would do that. The city didn't have the time or the resources to do it anyway. Microchipping or a rabies tag would do fine as identification. Animals didn't need to be registered in a database. It was a violation of privacy after all. All dogs in the city limits were required to have a rabies vaccination anyway, which could be traced to a vet.

Beatrice, catching herself slumping, suddenly sat up straight and pushed back the sting she felt in her lower back, an unconscious reminder of her mother's attempts to train Beatrice like one of her precious dogs. One of Beatrice's bad habits had always been slumping, always trying to make her gargantuan self smaller. Berta had always tried to break Beatrice of it, karate-chopping the small of Beatrice's back that was big even when Beatrice was little. Beatrice grimaced, remembering the pain and embarrassment, then took a sip of her coffee and tried to focus. *How would she word the most damaging finding of all?* The one that would put the final knife into Blackmon's need to regulate dog breeders--the dog breeder restrictions. Blackmon's proposed spay/neuter ordinance would also charge breeders for a license fee just to breed as well as charge them to keep a dog intact. It also regulated one yearly litter per dog. Dogs' gestation periods were six months, so most breeders usually bred their dogs twice a year, thus producing two litters yearly. This requirement, if passed, would cost the dog breeders money.

Beatrice had just received a hundred hits on her new blog, "You Can't Fix Irresponsible Pet Owners," which she had linked to research that cited reasons why spay and neuter laws wouldn't work. She had included the American Dog Club's fight against Blackmon's proposed spay/neuter ordinance, which had been posted on the club's website along with other legislation that the club thought affected them.

Beatrice was becoming big-time.

For the local business news website, Beatrice had even written some editorials that were garnering buzz. The editor had asked Beatrice to be a guest columnist on city issues. Her next editorial was working-titled: "Trash Talk and Why We Need It."

Blackmon, along with Councilwoman Meyers, of course, had vetoed automated trash for Beatrice's own neighborhood because the residents had complained how difficult it would be to wheel the new-fangled trashcans to the street in front of their homes for the trash men to pick up. They were used to having their trash picked up in their alleyway since cavemen rode in on dinosaurs to cart it away, like something out of a *Flintstone's* cartoon. Beatrice had talked to her neighbors, trying to convince them that automated trash service would be better, but many of them couldn't hear anyway, they so old and deaf. Beatrice was designing a citizen petition to ensure that automated trash in its final phase of implementation would be completed in all parts of the city. It was her duty to fulfill the plan that the city had okayed and the taxpayers had paid for, after all.

So angry from just thinking about it, Beatrice clamped her large hand over her mouth to stop her from cursing out loud. She glanced around the coffee shop to see if anyone had seen her, but they hadn't, which was unusual since Beatrice usually attracted looks by her size alone. She closed the laptop, placed it in her satchel and threw it over her shoulder before she got up and walked through the door to her Prius.

 Beatrice shuffled in her Birkenstock sandals through the automated doors of the new police station, where the Fortville City Council would meet. She saw a policewoman she knew sitting behind the front desk that she didn't want to see, so Beatrice tried to escape unnoticed through the community room doors, but that was difficult for big Beatrice.

 "Hey, Beatrice, what are you doing here?" Beatrice heard Kendra say.

 Beatrice froze. Kendra was a policewoman and a one-night stand that Beatrice had never called back. "City council," Beatrice said, tucking her chin into her ample bosom and clutching her satchel tighter under her arm.

 The other cop smirked as if he knew Beatrice's and Kendra's secret, the smirker being a dirty bicycle cop who had been punished by being slammed behind a desk after twenty-five years in the field. He had berated his wife in public at the

Mexican restaurant downtown, where he was working his beat, and, in return, his wife had thrown a margarita in his face before he could get away on his bicycle. It had made the local newspaper.

Beatrice stumbled through the community room door. She couldn't deal with this now.

The crowd was red. And big. Beatrice had never seen so many people at a City Council meeting. Beatrice thought she must have missed a memo and looked around, trying to figure out who all these people were and why they wore red t-shirts. The brand new community room, with its continuous desks going on forever like a sea of shiny woodgrain, was beautiful. Tonight, she was going to win. And she was going to smile. *She was going to be the big fish swimming around in a shining sea of woodgrain.*

It didn't take Beatrice long to find Dotty in the crowd, Dotty making a spectacle out of herself, waving her skinny arms around, trying to get Beatrice's attention. Dotty looked like a flag on a flagpole, all decked out in her patriotic sweater although it one of the hottest Augusts on record for Fortville.

"Did you get my text?" Dotty asked Beatrice while she fumbled into the seat Dotty had saved her. "Are you ready?

As the director of Homeless Angels, the local non-profit that helped feed and shelter Fortville's growing homeless population, an American Dog Club breeder herself and a member of the Fortville Humane Society, Dotty thought herself an invaluable resource regarding homeless dogs in area. Some of them, coincidentally, were owned by her very own homeless clients. But Beatrice, of course, had done all the research and writing for the report while Dotty just talked.

"I'm as ready as I'll ever be," Beatrice said, glancing at her cell phone barking a text alert. Beatrice looked at them. "Good job," read the first text. The second text, from Dotty, read, "Are you ready?" Beatrice noticed that Dotty had just sent hers when Beatrice had sat down. "Why don't you just ask me? I'm right here," Beatrice said, her deep voice starting to quiver a little from nervousness. She hoped Dotty didn't notice.

"I did just ask you," Dotty said, looking as if she had lost her best friend. "Anyway. Doesn't matter. You're going to do just fine tonight."

Dotty loved to text and had been doing it a lot. It made her feel conspiratorial, like she and Beatrice were the only ones privy to the technology, although texting had been mainstream for awhile.

"What's with the red?" Beatrice asked, looking at Dotty's red scarf.

"I don't know. I just happened to wear this," Dotty said, glancing behind her at the crowd, tightening the scarf around her pale skinny neck. The scarf reminded Beatrice of a rope noose like the ones the park rangers still hung at the Fortville gallows in commemoration of real-live hangings back in the late eighteen-hundreds. She hoped the red scarf wasn't an omen signifying some bad luck coming round the bend. "I guess it's some kind of holiday," Dotty continued. "It's not red anyway, it's *crimson*."

Beatrice checked her phone again and read the third text, which said, "L'Arion flipping his vote." Beatrice smiled even bigger as she studied the city leaders sitting behind a semi-circle of a desk on the podium.

Facing Beatrice, on her right, was Buddy Bateman, a retired man, without much of a spine and even less hair. Bateman had voted for the spay/neuter ordinance and would always vote for it.

After Bateman was L'Arion Middler, a Choctaw in dreadlocks who had voted for the spay/neuter ordinance the first time but had since changed his mind according to the text.

Third was Ron Fleming, a charismatic preacher with a flaming red goatee like the devil himself, which could be good or bad for business depending on how one looked at it. He had voted down the spay/neuter ordinance once and would forever veto it because that's what God had instructed him to do.

Next in line was Ralph Popodopolis, a Greek restaurant owner also known as Crazy Ralph because one never knew which way his vote would swing. Ralph had voted down the spay/neuter ordinance and would continue to vote it down because it was an election year.

Mayor Marion Bell (whose wife shared the same name but spelled it differently, a source of never-ending confusion) preceded Al Nosack, the city administrator with his slicked-back, used-car salesman hair. Although neither of these two would vote, they did exercise sway over the council members.

Next was Anne Meyers, tucked tightly into her white suit, sitting up prim and proper and looking at her cell phone. Meyers had and would always vote yes on the spay/neuter ordinance.

Then there sat Gary Rhodes. Gary, of course, a smart man, had voted it down and would always vote it down. Beatrice smiled at him and then pretended to look at her phone while Gary smiled back. Beatrice hoped he wasn't flirting with her. Beatrice was unsure if she even liked women, let alone men. Beatrice looked over at Dotty, who was especially frazzled today. She tried to remember their love connection but couldn't recall much beyond the empty wineglasses under the comforter the morning after their first hook-up several years ago.

But Beatrice did know that she loved dogs. Good, well-made dogs with perfect temperaments. She thought of poor Martina lying in her grave, those bastard shelter dogs running over the top of it.

Beatrice eyed Councilman Lance Blackmon, who was last but not least in the city leader line-up, and thought his left eye was already beginning to quiver.

Lily-Chapter Seven

    The Lady with Sad Eyes had gone away and left Lily alone in the room where Lily had slept the night before, the tall water bowl towering in the corner. The little Chinese-Crested wondered why she had been left with no friends and wished The Lady with Sad Eyes would come back. The Man with Old Eyes could stay away though. Lily didn't particularly like him. Those funny shiny circles running round his eyes scared her to death.
    Through the door, Lily could hear Buster whining. Buster was Lily's new friend with the puffy white chest

and funny eyes that bulged. Lily supposed the other dogs were on the opposite side of the door and lying on the big fluffy bed. It wasn't fair.

The little dog flipped on her back and drew circles in the air with her fringed paws. She was feeling bored but amorous, which was unusual for the savvy, single dog who usually played it cool regarding relationships.

Once, she had a boyfriend named Julio, but he, with his dark hair and eyes, was a bit of a rapscallion chasing after the other dogs. Lily tried to imagine the boring Buster as her boyfriend but could not, Lily preferring a run for her money.

Buster, frustrated, began digging under the door, his sharp claws making a racket on the tile floor. Lily rolled over and put her head between her paws to get a better view of *The Buster Show.* She wanted to be near Buster like the night before, wrapped in his big paws. She felt safe with him, like when she was a puppy nestled between her brothers and sisters, nudging them over for a suckle. But Buster, to Lily, was a brother like Fredo, nothing more.

Lily stood up and looked around her, trying to find a distraction, her little beady eyes finally landing on a roll of paper beside the tall water bowl. She remembered from last night The Man with Old Eyes sitting atop the tall water bowl, tearing pieces from the roll and wiping his tail with them. She figured The Lady with Sad Eyes wouldn't be mad at her for doing the same.

Lily flung her little body at the tall water bowl, trying to reach the roll, balancing on her little hind legs, jumping hard as she could, leveraging her front paws over the rim of the tall water bowl.

But she kept slipping.

So she jumped again.

Lily lost her balance and tumbled backward, landing on her back, the breath knocked out of her. When she opened her eyes, Lily saw curtains dancing in a breeze reeking of the old bulldog that had snapped at her that morning. Lily could even smell his bone, which smelled so good that Lily made up her mind to take it away from him as soon as she could. Lily's newest world was ready and waiting for her right through that open window if she could only reach it.

Determined, Lily rolled over and crawled back onto her little legs. She inhaled deep and again flung herself upon the tall water bowl, pushing her hind legs out from under her, jumping as high as she could, getting her little forepaws to just over the edge but not quite enough to hoist herself over the top.

Lily jumped and climbed and jumped and climbed, getting up and falling down again and again, until she finally leveraged her little body over the top of the tall water bowl and into...a very cold bowl of water!

She splashed and sputtered until her little legs began to churn then paddled for a few moments until, exhausted, Lily, preparing for the end of her short doggy life, let her paws drop. Finding herself actually standing in the toilet bowl, she peeked her pointed, speckled nose just over the edge and spied the window again. Lily took a deep breath and jumped toward the window, using the roll of paper like a springboard to scramble onto the vanity. Lily caught her breath and stopped for a moment, savoring her success, enjoying her new, taller perspective and looked around.

Buster was still clawing under the door and howling. Lily felt a little bit sorry for him but only for a moment, prompting the very wet Lily to bark back, telling Buster not to worry and that she would return with The Lady with Sad Eyes. Lily had already bounced out of the window onto the grass before Buster whined back his response.

On Lily's way past the bulldog, Jake, he woofed at her nicely, informing Lily that his bone was hers if she would stay and visit him. But Lily had no time to eat or socialize because she was on a mission to find The Lady with Sad Eyes who had saved her. Lily had no interest in a silly bone or a silly bulldog and ran fast toward the sunset.

Morgan-Chapter 8

The McAfees were driving to Fortville for a City Council meeting Derril had asked them to attend and Ray, as usual, wouldn't stop with the talking and questioning.

"I don't know what to expect tonight or what's going on," Morgan responded, trying her best not to be short. "I just know that Derril needs our help."

Through the dirty passenger window of the McAfee's diesel Dually, Morgan looked at the naked fields, the corn and soybean crops gleaned, the dry, barren earth flitting past. The sun, lazy in the western sky, tuckered after his long day of shining, was poised to cast some golden bewitchery upon the flat land of the Arkansas River bottoms. Morgan hated "going into town," as her mother always called it. Fortville was a much bigger town with much more important folks than Multown. She wished she was back at home, sitting in front of her computer, the inside dogs curled around her.

Morgan spent every evening on the computer, emailing the volunteers with instructions on pound protocol or designating the assignments for the upcoming benefit, but most importantly, and which the benefit made possible, finding the dogs temporary or permanent homes.

If she were home, all of her house dogs would be asleep, except Lily, who would probably be in Morgan's lap, if not on the keyboard, trying to capture Morgan's attention all for herself. Ray, worn-out from his day of dogs and dentistry, would be in the den in front of the blaring television, probably asleep.

Morgan's keen power of persuasion, untapped until opening the animal shelter, had formed an efficient network of dog-loving volunteers, who helped Morgan do what she had neither the time nor talent to do.

After a dog came into the shelter, either Morgan or a photographer would take photos of it. Then Morgan would send those photos to two retired school teachers, both by-the-book English grammarians. They would give the dogs interesting names like Reese or Flynn and write charming biographies of mostly fiction to match since the dogs' pasts were unknowable or just too sad to publish.

People who wanted to adopt a dog would use PetFinder, a search engine, which was linked to the McAfee Mutts website. Most were looking for a specific breed of dog, but some were just browsing with no pet prerequisites. The search engine had been responsible for most of the adoptions.

Recently, Derril, who was tech-savvy, had put the shelter on Facebook, which had generated a lot of social buzz but, so far, no adoptions. Morgan had neither the time nor temperament to keep up with "all that gab" on Facebook.

Word of mouth resulted in a few *but very few* adoptions.

Morgan preferred the distance that on-line communication gave her, avoiding in-person contact with the potential adopter until Morgan was sure he or she was a perfect guardian for a McAfee Mutt. Applicants, vetted like potential employees, had to fill out detailed on-line applications that included peer and vet referrals. Morgan also required potential adopters to sign papers authorizing impromptu at-home visits before, during and/or after adoption. Most animal welfare organizations lacked either the resources or the willingness to ensure excellent homes for their adoptable animals.

Morgan didn't give her dogs away making it a privilege to adopt a McAfee Mutt. Adoption fees depended on medical attention administered when readying a dog for adoption. All animals, of course, were spayed and neutered.

Morgan saw a greasy spot on the road's shoulder.

"What's that?" Morgan said under her breath. Ray, late for the City Council meeting, sped toward it. Morgan looked at Ray, hoping he was going on about something halfway interesting. He was wearing his new wire frame glasses, which made him like younger, more like in his hippy days, like John Lennon if you squinted a bit. She tried to concentrate on what Ray was saying, but he sounded like a Charlie Brown parent and nothing like John Lennon. His blather was never ending.

So Morgan looked back at the road. But it was only a dead possum. Or a big dead white rat, she couldn't quite tell. Lying on its back, the body bloated and twisted, its legs and skinny tail askew, its snout pointing toward Heaven. Morgan didn't believe in Heaven but hoped there was one, and the poor dead thing was in it munching on grub worms. She hoped it wasn't an omen. If that were the case, Morgan would never have any luck, what with the scores of dead animals on Oklahoma highways.

Suddenly, Morgan laughed deep from her gut, conjuring a rawness that surprised and shocked her. Morgan used to look for animals that needed her help. Now she avoided them.

"What's so funny?" Ray asked.

"I was just happy that it was a dead possum on the side of the road instead of a dead dog. Or a hurt dog."

"County should pick that up," Ray said, pushing up his new oval wire-frames. "We pay taxes for that.

Those boys better get on it." He grimaced. "These glasses you picked out for me don't work."

Morgan smiled, her down-turned eyes curving upward for a split second, and reached over and patted Ray's arm, still muscled from all its dog doings despite sixty-two years of gravity. "I'm sorry. But they look nice on you. I'll get them worked on. Did you get the hole in the fence fixed?"

"Yep."

That morning Morgan had captured all twenty of the four-legged escapees after spending two hours collecting them, some of the passersby getting out of their car to help. She had herded the dogs into the air-conditioned shed along with its regular occupants. The guy in the car accident was okay, too, although she barely remembered him. She was much more concerned with the dogs' safety than any human's.

When she had gotten home after work, Morgan had forgotten to see if Ray had fixed the fence and the dogs were back in their yard that faced the highway. She tried not to think about the mess that twenty plus animals would leave in the small room.

Morgan had also put Lily back in the bathroom where Lily had slept the night before because the little dog hadn't been spade yet and was in heat. Ray hadn't had the opportunity to take her to the spay/neuter clinic. He did that on Thursdays, his day off from work. It was only Tuesday.

"Did you let the dogs back into their outside area after you got the fence fixed?" Morgan asked, trying to twist her hair, an old habit from when she had time to have hair long enough to twist.

Ray paused for a moment, thinking. "Yeah, I think so."

"Did you get that other dog, the one at the office, to the shelter?"

"Yep."

That afternoon, someone had abandoned a collie mix on a leash and attached it to the dental office's backdoor. In between dental appointments and on his way to one of his many chores, Ray had flung open the door and jerked the poor dog, leash and all, into the hallway. Scared and shaking, the dog had peed on Ray's brand-new white tennis shoes.

"You're twisting your hair again," Ray said, catapulting Morgan, lost in her dog world, back to him. "Or trying to. You don't even have long enough hair to do that. You haven't done that in a long time."

Morgan's short, spiky hair was still damp from the shower she had taken after getting home from the office. She had scrambled to find a red t-shirt and could only find an old one, silver balloon letters spelling *TIGER* across the front of it. She had gotten it in a garage sale and worn it until it was thin and stretchy, naturally distressed by Morgan and the many dogs she had put it through. She needed familiarity and comfort for this meeting tonight. She had Ray. He always made her feel loved and secure. But she really needed some confidence. Surely the meeting would go well.

The Fortville City Council would, of course, make it law for dog owners to sterilize their dogs. Breeders could still breed dogs but would have to be licensed and pay a fee. How could they protest that? All they needed to do was visit her one day at the shelter to understand how important it was for people to keep their pets from breeding and adding to the millions of homeless animals. *It should be a law.* Maybe, just maybe, it could help ease the suffering of all the dogs that had to be killed because there weren't enough homes in all the world for them. And what about the people's souls, like hers, that were murdered over and over, hundreds of times, putting those unwanted dogs to death.

Don't breed or buy while shelter dogs die. It was on her business card. It should be on every billboard. That afternoon, Morgan had had to put six dogs to sleep. One of them was the white schnauzer, Buddy, who was just too old. When Buddy closed his one good eye for the last time, Morgan had cried for the first time since starting the shelter.

Morgan looked at the backs of the people in the crowded community room and was thankful she saw red. One of the volunteers had sent an email asking people to wear red to show support for the proposed spay/neuter ordinance. The volunteers had come. Lots of them. Morgan had only had a few human friends in her life. Her brother had been her friend, but he was gone now, dead of AIDS. The animals were all she had ever needed. For Morgan, the volunteers were the closest she had to human friends.

"Morgan, hey, over here," Morgan heard a just-a-little-too-loud voice say. It was Derril in a very-wrinkled, red-knit shirt. "They just got started." Derril's mother must have missed seeing Derril leave in that shirt;

otherwise, she would not have let him out of the house wearing it. Derril's mother, whom he still lived with, still ironed his clothes.

Morgan hated being late but taking care of so many animals never gave her a choice. Derril moved manila folders out of the padded chairs that he had saved for Morgan and Ray, who sat down, trying not to make a fuss. Morgan felt a hundred eyes upon her while her old pal, insecurity, got the go-ahead. Morgan glanced down at the word *TIGER* written across her chest, hoping it would inject some courage into her. So far, it wasn't working.

"Take a look at these," Derril said, looking over his bright purple cat-eye reading glasses, his gray-green eyes bugged open as usual. Regretfully, Derril had been born that way. Derril was also a bit of an eccentric. Although he was not an attractive man, he had a great smile and strong chipmunk cheeks that could chop a two-by-four in half. Morgan had met Derril when he had adopted Sandy, a rat terrier. Derril handed the folders to Morgan and Ray.

"How are the pups?" Morgan asked, opening the folder.

"They're ready to go if I can let them go," Derril replied. He always fostered a few dogs for Morgan despite his mother's pleas to stop. His mother did not like their messes though Derril always cleaned them up.

"What are these?" Morgan asked, looking at the the paper inside the folder.

"The numbers," Derril said. "Take a look."

On the papers were scrawls and scribbles and a number circled at the bottom of each column of hand-written figures. Morgan made out that it was the number of dogs and cats euthanized at the Fortville Animal Shelter.

"This is for what year?" Morgan asked, assuming the data was old.

"Last year," Derril said, shaking his head. "Can you believe it?"

The Fortville Humane Society, which ran the Fortville Animal Shelter, was putting to sleep more animals despite the two spay/neuter clinics that had been opened in the area in the past couple of years.

At that shelter, Morgan had witnessed her first euthanasia, a painful experience that had inspired her to leave there seven years ago to start her own shelter.

The death was unnecessarily cruel, with no sedative administered before the euthanasia drugs were injected. The little dog had been frantic as a big man held it down on the dirty exam table, the dog's legs flailing while another person waved a syringe around, trying to locate the little dog's tiny vein and plunge the needle into it.

Since that time, Morgan had performed plenty of euthanasias, making sure they were nothing like that horror. She could usually do them by herself. With bigger, stronger or feral dogs, she would call Ray to help her. Morgan always used a sedative, which she purchased herself, to calm the dog first.

"These terrible statistics will help us get the spay/neuter ordinance passed," whispered Derril.

"How did you get these?" Morgan whispered back.

Derril hesitated for a moment, which was unusual since Derril charged headlong into most everything. "They're public record since the money it takes to collect them and house them and kill them or find them homes is from us, the taxpayer."

The shelter was so overwhelmed with thousands of animals to care for by an overworked staff that it had become a cold, cruel beast that chewed up its victims, both animals and people, and spat them back out. People, who were irresponsible with their pets by allowing them to breed indiscriminately, had birthed not only thousands of puppies but a vicious bitch of a mother who couldn't take care of them all.

It was best the public, who paid for it, didn't know the truth, which was hard to hear. When the statistics were published, it always made for an uproar of finger-pointing with no one, certainly not the animals, winning.

Morgan knew the Fortville Humane Society didn't even publish their euthanasia records, although she thought they should.

Morgan continued to grill Derril. "Did you go and get them? Did you call them? Who did you speak to?"

Morgan had met Donna Martelli, the Fortville Humane Society's director, years ago. Morgan had recruited Donna to protest a circus. They had even dressed up like clowns. Morgan had gotten Donna interested in animal welfare. Morgan looked around for Donna but didn't see her, Morgan wondering why she wasn't there to show her support. Donna was probably too tired. But so was Morgan.

"I think its important to know what the stats are that's all," Derril said, looking down at the paper.

"Actually, I got them from him." Derril shrugged his shoulders and motioned toward an older gentleman in the front row, a man with beautiful fluffy white hair topping his head like a cumulus cloud.

"Do you know who he is, Derril?" Morgan asked.

"No," Derril said a little too loudly, shaking his head. "People want to talk first before the directors vote, to tell them how they're feeling about this spay/neuter ordinance. Now, shhhhhh..."

Morgan thought Derril should shush himself.

The man in the middle of the City Council, a man that resembled Colonel Sanders of the fried chicken franchises but dressed in a green suit and tie instead, tapped his microphone a few times. "Before we vote on these animal ordinances," he said, reading from a computer tablet, "a few people have signed up to talk about them. Plus, we have a report from the animal committee leader, Beatrice Cooper," he continued, never looking up.

Morgan recognized Lance Blackmon, the city councilman, sitting on the end. He was a volunteer for her and had helped her find homes for several dogs, adopting several black labs, black dogs hardly ever adopted, himself. He had done much for the animal community, but his left eye was twitching, which was strange. Morgan had never noticed that before.

Colonel Sanders droned on. "Beatrice was assigned to find out the practicality of these new animal ordinances that have been proposed. And we think she's done a fine job. She has thirteen recommendations for the council to vote on." Morgan looked at the name plaque beside the man who was talking. His name was Mayor Marion Bell, who nodded, somewhat painfully, toward the front row. "But, Mr. Sterling, you're first."

The man whom Derril had pointed out, the one who had given out the euthanasia stats, the one with the puffy cloud on his head, walked slowly to the podium. He stood in front of it, facing the city leaders with his back to the crowd.

He was a small man who seemed even smaller with his large white head of unruly curly hair. He wore old-fashioned, faded Wrangler jeans and a reddish denim shirt, a red patch on his left shoulder, the shirt pressed and starched so many times it was faded. He had a Western belt with his name, *Billy Bob*, leather-tooled into the back of it, which reminded Morgan of her shop class in high school where she made a leather belt because the shop teacher wouldn't allow her to learn about cars.

"You're on the clock, Billy Bob," said Col. Sanders, jokingly, though no one in the room laughed. Morgan assumed Billy Bob wasn't laughing either.

Billy Bob slowly cleared his throat like he had all the time in the world. Then he cleared it again just to make sure everyone heard him clear it if they hadn't heard it the first time. "I am Billy Bob Sterling, owner of Sterling Trailer Sales and the director of a low-cost spay/neuter clinic in Fortville," said his deep, throaty voice that drifted like a slow river from the podium. "At a spay/neuter conference I went to, I found out that at a Stockholm, Sweden, shelter, they euthanized five out of five-hundred dogs they collected with most of the five-hundred dogs returned to their owners. Well, we asked them what their secret was. They said that they teach their citizens personal responsibility -- not laws."

Billy Bob stopped for a moment, looked up from the paper then glanced at the City Council. Most of them were ignoring him, more entranced with their computer tablets, except for the councilwoman and Lance, who was trying to reciprocate but couldn't, his left eye twitching so.

"I agree it would be better to educate the public to spay or neuter their dogs," Billy Bob continued, "to bring them around to voluntarily spaying or neutering their pet. But there's no time for that while more and more animals are killed. I don't think our residents think about what actually happens to an animal when it goes into a shelter. I don't know if the council here knows how much we're paying to the Fortville Humane Society per animal. You may be surprised to find out how much it is. It's fifteen dollars a day for a dog or cat."

Billy Bob shook his head as if waiting for a response. Getting none, he looked back at his paper. "Approximately seventy-six percent of the animals that this shelter took in last year were euthanized. This town spends six-hundred thousand a year alone for animal control run by our city police and a shelter with a humane society to run it. If we passed this law, we would have to house and euthanize a lot less homeless animals, which would save all of us, the taxpayers, a lot of money."

Like fans at a football game, a red wave rolled across the room, people in red shirts standing and clapping. Billy Bob turned and smiled, waving at the crowd, looking as if he might blow a kiss, but he did not.

The mayor droned that Billy Bob was running out of time. Billy Bob slammed his fist down on the podium, causing the crowd to jump. "But it's not about the right thing or the wrong thing to do, it's just about doing *something*. Passing the spay/neuter ordinance is doing *something*. Thank you."

Morgan turned and looked at Ray, who was asleep sitting up, his head lolled over to the side and his new glasses teetered at the end of his nose.

Morgan jabbed Ray in his side. "Clap, Ray."

Which Ray did, half asleep.

Col. Sanders droned on again. "Next up, we have Beatrice Cooper."

Morgan glanced at Lance, who had become a bit of a spectacle, removing his black glasses and wiping his left eye with a tissue given to him by the pretty councilwoman. Morgan had never noticed his eye going on like that, blinking, blinking. She hoped it would stop. It made her want to twist her hair again.

Morgan watched the monolith of a woman named Beatrice slowly stand up, her enormity casting a shadow over the room. Beatrice tugged up her skinny black jeans, her white underwear peeking over the waistband. She pulled down her black t-shirt as her jeans worked their way south again. Beatrice tucked her laptop under her arm while a skinny blonde woman in a red scarf sitting beside her reached over and, just missing Beatrice's waist, patted Beatrice's healthy bottom instead.

Beatrice, seemingly nonplussed by the bottom incident, trudged her way to the lectern with her head down. Morgan wondered how the very large woman could see without looking where she was going. Beatrice raised up the microphone, opened her laptop on the lectern and punched a few keys on the keyboard. Beatrice had to lean over to see her laptop screen, causing her black t-shirt to ride up again and her jeans to repeat their way down, her white underwear making an encore. She wiggled her healthy backside toward the audience, hoisting up her jeans with her massive fingers looped through her belt loops. Morgan thought that Beatrice must have a hard time finding clothes to fit her...or even a car.

"My name is Beatrice Cooper," the tall, very large woman read from the laptop monitor, her deep voice quivering. "And I was on the animal committee that was commissioned by the City of Fortville to determine if mandating spay/neuter would be feasible and thus lower the homeless pet overpopulation in Fortville."

Morgan ventured that Beatrice, though she had only witnessed the backside of her, was what one might call a handsome woman. She imagined Beatrice would have been home on the range, perhaps driving cattle or heading a marshall's posse. Morgan wondered how Beatrice could fit into life these days, her so big and life so small.

Beatrice cleared her throat uncomfortably and projected an American Dog Club logo on the screen. "Our first findings come from the American Dog Club which says mandatory spay/neuter laws have proven to be ineffective." She pointed at the screen with her long finger. "Numerous studies have found they result in significant cost increases and many other unintended consequences for responsible dog owners, local shelters and the community at large without addressing the real underlying issue of irresponsible dog ownership." Beatrice pulled up her pants again while Morgan wondered what the American Dog Club had to do with spaying and neutering.

Beatrice brought up some more logos with an X through the words *mandatory spay/neuter* and paused for a moment. "For these reasons, the American Dog Club is joined by the National Vet Association and the Society Against Animal Cruelty in opposing mandatory sterilization policies."

Morgan unable to believe what she was hearing, staved an overwhelming urge to jump up and curse this big woman, although she wasn't usually a curser. The red crowd gasped.

Beatrice continued, her voice growing bigger. "The only thing these spay/neuter laws will do is punish people who already take good care of their dogs by making them pay breeder fees or getting their dogs fixed. Most people probably would spay/neuter their dogs if they weren't a dog breeder," Beatrice waved her big hand. "Plus, it would also be costly to enforce a spay/neuter law too. The animal control officers here are already tasked enough with what they have to do. How can they enforce a spay/ neuter law as well?"

Beatrice stopped, took a deep breath, and punched a few buttons on her computer keyboard, projecting a photo of a signed document on the screen. "Twenty local vets have signed a paper saying that mandating spay and neuter would not solve the problem. They are the ones that would know," she said, her voice gaining momentum. "We also believe that more people would give up their pets to the shelter because they couldn't afford to have them fixed if a spay/neuter ordinance were passed. We have more in our report. There are thirteen recommendations regarding city animal care and control, which we gave to the City Council. Nixing the spay/neuter ordinance is only one of them."

The room was quiet. Morgan noticed Lance was now squinting through his right eye only, his left eye, apparently, worn out and shut tight.

"Thank you," Beatrice said, closing her laptop then grabbing it off the podium. "Oh, I almost forgot. Check out my blog at *You Can't Fix Irresponsible Pet Owners.*" Beatrice hoisted up her jeans again then let go to salute the City Council with one of her big hands. It was all that Morgan could do to not laugh when Beatrice's jeans proceeded to fall down again.

Col. Mayor Sanders tapped his microphone while Beatrice, the human Rottweiler, walked back to her chair. "Thanks Beatrice," the mayor said in his mind-numbing monotone. "We appreciate it. Now let's take a vote on each of the animal service task force's thirteen recommendations."

Morgan noticed Derril and Ray were staring at her. "What is it you want me to do?" Morgan asked, pressing her index fingers against her temple, feeling a headache coming on. "I don't have time for this. It's all I can do to take care of the animals I have now. That Beatrice is an idiot."

Derril opened the manila folder and looked up and down again at the statistics, his purple reading glasses pushed up on his head, his grey roots winning the war against Grecian Formula. "Over seventy-six percent of the homeless animals are killed every year in this town. I know what I can do," Derril said in a matter-of-fact voice like the deal was done. "I can join that new permanent animal board that's forming. They could use our perspective from a rescue."

That sounded like a good idea to Morgan. She had read about the new animal board that was forming but didn't have any time for it. It couldn't hurt for Derril to join. It would be good to have a McAfee Mutt volunteer on that panel of people. Maybe they could get something done. More and more animals were dying every day because there were not enough homes.

Morgan was doing everything she could. Derril would only help her mission.

Beatrice-Chapter 9

At the Tulsa Dog Show, Beatrice watched Dotty take Pesto around the show ring for what was, hopefully, the final round, before the judge would award the Italian greyhound the grand champion prize.

Pesto was competing against Cha-Cha's Champion, a black Afghan hound, with long ebony hair, that had lived up to her name by nabbing the top spot at the show for three years running. But, today, Cha-Cha was opting to sit and look out into space instead.

On the other hand, little Pesto was positively on fire.

Dorothea's Italian Stallion, Pesto's registered name, cocked his nose up high in the air, his little stocking feet moving under him like a compact brindle blur of dog poetry, and glided around the ring.

To teach Pesto to gait in the American Dog Club-deemed way with the dog moving his right front leg forward while moving his left back leg forward then vice-versa, Dotty had wrapped tiny ankle weights around Pesto's legs when training him. The residual effect was that the little dog walked around as if perpetually trying out for The Rockettes.

And though the training method might have been questionable, the results were certainly paying off. The critical dog show patrons were enthusiastically cheering Pesto, who was high-stepping around the ring like a four-legged, goose-stepping Nazi, loving the attention.

Dotty had felt so guilty about putting weights on Pesto's legs that she had also donned a pair of leg weights herself while training the Italian greyhound, thus transforming her skinny calves into sexy, curvy legs that she was showing off any chance she got.

Now Dotty, at forty-two, in orthopedic shoes, nude panty hose, black leather miniskirt and a red-white-

and-blue t-shirt, pranced right along with Pesto on the leash beside her. Pesto had been a little depressed at the loss of Martina, his first and last lay, but if Pesto's behavior today was any indicator, he was coming out of his funk.

Earlier in the day at the dog show, while Beatrice and Dotty were talking, Pesto, hardly ever venturing too far from Dotty, had sneaked away to a female bulldog who caught his attention. But the stocky little bulldog had called Pesto's bluff and mounted the Italian greyhound instead, just about killing poor Pesto when the little dog's legs were knocked out from under him. Pesto lay prone, his nose-planted into the parquet floor of the dog grooming area.

"At least he's upped his ante from the mops he likes to dry hump," Dotty had said to Beatrice after collecting the crumpled little dog and clipping him back on his leash.

Beatrice, however, wasn't getting over Martina as quickly.

Rihanna and Bay-Bay were having a hard time of it, too, both lying at Beatrice's big Birkenstocked feet like two anorexic, grieving widows, while, from the bleachers, Beatrice watched the dog show. Dotty had wanted to put the girls in Spanish mantillas, but Beatrice forbade it. She hated dogs dressed in costumes, thinking it disrespected their fine pedigrees.

"Go, Pesto. Show them how it's done," Beatrice yelled, trying to be supportive but wishing it was she and Martina in the ring instead. "Go, Dotty."

In honor of the dog show, Beatrice had traded in her black t-shirt for a more festive white one, an Italian greyhound silk-screened upon it. Although Beatrice and Dotty had taken the day off, Beatrice was working on her laptop, hoping she had enough battery power to finish her blog about last night's City Council meeting. Beatrice wanted to blog about the automated trash controversy, but Fortville just couldn't couldn't get off this stupid spay/neuter business.

She still couldn't believe the Fortville City Council had tabled the spay/neuter ordinance for seven months after all the hard work she had done trying to refute it. By a very familiar four-to-three vote, the four votes from the same council members who would've voted against the spay/neuter ordinance last night, had passed her recommendation that pet spay/neuter must be *encouraged* rather than *mandated*. That councilwoman Meyers, too afraid the animal ordinance, with its spay/neuter ordinance in it, would be voted down last night, had tabled the animal ordinance vote while Blackmon, holding a tissue up to his eye, seconded her motion. The vote would've been three for it and four against it. Then one more vote, in two weeks, and it would've been dead. This stupid tabling, like a slow euthanasia, just held off the inevitable mercy killing.

But the Fortville leaders did approve a nine-member animal board, Beatrice's idea, to replace her animal committee, which had finished its job. The permanent board would advise the City Council on animal-related matters. Two would be veterinarians, one would represent livestock, two would stand for non-profit animal interest groups and would be required to be on their board of directors. Four members had to be Fortville residents.

Last night, regretfully, the City Council had passed only eleven of Beatrice's thirteen recommendations. Unapproved were her recommendations that roaming cats had to be spayed and neutered along with the regular feeding of stray animals constituting their adoption. The vote was ludicrous. If Fortville wanted to become a feral cat Wild Kingdom, so be it. More feral cats than feral humans were in Fortville, she supposed, although the count was close.

Her blog would refute what stupid Billy Bob Sterling had said about Stockholm last night, about it being such a great place for animals since they had such a low euthanasia rate.

This was true; however, Beatrice had found Stockholm didn't even have mandatory spay/neuter ordinances but, instead, fell under Swedish animal welfare laws that encouraged all animals to be treated well. Dogs couldn't even be crated unless it was for special reasons such as for dog shows or trips. The Swedes even encouraged people to spend time with their dogs twice a day. In fact, what Billy Bob had said only proved Beatrice's point: People needed to be educated--not forced--to fix their dogs.

Beatrice finished typing her piece then accessed the stadium's wi-fi, punching in a key strokes with her big fingers, cracking the code. She pressed "send" and waited to hear the swoosh that indicated her email was on its way, then closed her laptop.

She hoped her business editor would like her editorial. Beatrice had never written much nor had an opinion about much of anything before. But someone had to take up for the people of Fortville. After all, how many more laws and lies could they take? Plus, Big Berta was also proud of Beatrice for fighting for dog owners' rights. That was a first. Her mother had never been proud of Beatrice for much of anything.

Beatrice watched while the judge stacked Pesto, the dog on a platform. Dotty offered Pesto some bait, otherwise known as a dog biscuit to lay people, trying to entice the little dog to hold up his head, a sign of alertness, which, surprisingly, Pesto did. Normally, his usual modus operandi was cowering and ducking.

But when the judge began checking out Pesto's privates, Pesto bit the judge squarely on the bulbous tip of her nose, making it bleed so profusely that the judge fainted and fell on Pesto. The whole platform and Pesto went crashing down. Dotty jumped out of the way just in time, yanking Pesto's leash with her, almost breaking his little neck.

From the bleachers, Beatrice stood up slowly, hoisting up her jeans, her mouth gaping open. She watched paramedics strap the dog judge in a gurney and wheel her out while Dotty, shaking her frizzy-blonde head, looked on in disbelief, Pesto cradled in her arms.

Beatrice felt the bleachers shaking and sat down to steady herself. She thought it might be her nerves but noticed Bay-Bay and Rihanna were also trembling a bit more than usual. Beatrice felt a large hand on her shoulder and turned around.

It was Ben, Beatrice's twin brother. "Hey, Sis, what just happened?" Ben, his mouth gaped open as widely as Beatrice's, pointing toward the show ring.

"Oh, gosh, Ben, you scared me to death," Beatrice said, shaking her head, relieved.

Ben was as big as Beatrice, if not bigger, the bleachers groaning from his weight. He, also a dog fancier like Beatrice, liked to come and watch the dog shows and had even shown his dogs a few times.

"Hey, brother," Beatrice said, turning and hugging Ben, trying not to smile and show off her teeth since Ben didn't have the funds to get his own teeth worked on. "What's going on?" Beatrice motioned toward the bleacher with her big hand. "Sit down."

Ben shifted on his seat and the bleachers groaned again, while the lady in front of them jumped up and scurried down a few rows, afraid the two might crash down upon her. "Came to watch Pesto perform," Ben said.

"Well, what do you think so far?"

"Doesn't look so good."

"Sure doesn't," Beatrice shook her head again. "And we were so close this year." Beatrice turned and examined her brother, who looked a bit down. Ben was usually in pretty good spirits. "Why didn't you show your dogs today?"

"No. Not today," Ben said, hesitating. "The dogs just aren't...ready."

Ben and Beatrice had grown up showing dogs. They had been practically born in a show ring and had learned how to stack a dog before they could walk. "Beatrice and Ben were whelped, not born," Big Berta loved to say.

Beatrice often imagined herself and Ben, like a couple of wolf babies, suckling at Big Berta's teats. Their childhood had not been idyllic since the twins' father had left them when they were just infants. When learning to walk, Beatrice and Ben had pulled themselves up with the help of Big Berta's first Bernese mountain dog, Griselda. Big Berta had tied the twins to the dog with a nylon rope around their waists.

"Did mother come?" Ben asked.

"No, the wolf mother couldn't tear herself away from her cubs," Beatrice said, screwing up her lips, simulating a smile. "They cubs were feeding."

Ben tried to smile but was self conscious of his teeth and rightly so, his choppers almost as brown as his eyes, which were always smiling and kind instead. But today was an exception. "How come Big Berta didn't make it?" Ben asked.

"Hilda was having her puppies today. Mother was staying home today to make sure they would be okay. What's the deal with your dogs? I thought they were ready to show."

"Me, too," Ben said, looking away and back at the show ring. "Maybe next year. I hope so. Looks like they're going to make an announcement."

Beatrice and Ben both leaned forward while the lady who had moved down a few bleachers glanced back at them.

A gentleman in a suit took the microphone and announced that the winner was Cha-Cha, who didn't act a bit excited, a bull mastiff getting all her attention instead. Pesto took reserve, which so surprised Dotty that she lifted Pesto in the air, twirling him above her head, but lost her balance and tripped on a toy poodle, hurling Pesto into the grandstands, where he just missed hitting a patron.

"I swear, that judge must've had some bait in her hand," Dotty said from the passenger side of Beatrice's Prius. Beatrice was driving them back to Fortville after the dog show. "That's why Pesto bit her nose."

"Or, more likely," Beatrice volleyed, "that judge had some bait up her nose."

They both laughed. Beatrice thought she had been quite funny today, despite her blues.

The dogs were all asleep in their crates in the backseat. Dotty had given poor banged-up Pesto and herself a doggy valium to calm them both down a bit. She had also offered one to Beatrice, who rejected pills of any kind.

While Dotty slept with her fuzzy hair crunched under noise-canceling headphones, Beatrice mulled the reasons why Ben hadn't shown his dogs, both recently taking prizes, making his decision not to show today even more unusual.

Ben and his wife, Reba, had been having some problems in their marriage, and Ben's job at the local tire store wasn't going all that great. After all, how great could it be selling tires? And his wife, Reba, was as mean as a snake.

    Beatrice accessed her email via the car's Bluetooth and looked at them on the car's computer screen. One of the e-mails was from Fortville city boss Al Nosack, so she opened it, wondering what he could want. It was a list of recent applicants for her animal board.

    One of the applicants was someone named Derril Harmon, a Fortville resident who volunteered for McAfee Mutts in Multown. This Derril wasn't even on a Fortville animal-service board from the looks of his resume. "Why are they even entertaining him as a potential candidate?" Beatrice said out loud, unconscious her inner voice had become a very loud outer voice. "He simply will not do. My dogs would do a better job. Well, *Martina*, anyway." Then Beatrice remembered that Martina was dead. "Stupid city." She glanced over at Dotty to see if Dotty had heard her, but Dotty was snoring as loud as her outfit. Beatrice had wanted Dotty to apply for the animal board, but Dotty had said no, claiming she had been under too much stress lately. Beatrice was a little upset with her decision since Dotty was the one who had gotten her into this mess.

Beatrice commanded the navigator to click off her email and turn on the radio. Pachelbel's *Canon*, her favorite song, was playing on NPR. Beatrice tried to concentrate on the music but couldn't and thought other thoughts instead. She was calling Al Nosack first thing in the morning. How dare he mess up her rules for applying to the animal board. So what if he was city administrator. Big deal.

Lily-Chapter 10

Lily jumped out of the bathroom window and barely missed Jake, the bulldog, lying underneath. But that didn't phase the little dog, who kept right on running as quick as her legs would go. Faster and faster she flew on her mission to find The Lady with Sad Eyes until a fence stopping her, the little dog came to a screeching halt, wondering what to do. She didn't want to dally because The Lady with Sad Eyes was still missing, out there somewhere. Suddenly, Lily heard a bark and looked back. Jake and several of his slobbering buddies were coming after her. Fast.

Lily heard a tiny squeak and perked high her tufted ears to hear it better, whipping around her fine head. On the other side of the fence was The Smallest Dog Ever, even smaller than Lily, the little thing standing on its little hind legs, twitching its little flat pink nose and flashing its little beady eyes, wringing its little paws, trying to tell her something.

It scurried along the fence line, running back and forth like a speeding ball of fur similar to the ones that Tom, The Yellow-Striped Skinny Dog, would cough up. Lily, her little head bouncing back and forth, watched the furry speedball until it disappeared. She wondered where it had gone until it popped up beside her, the little thing squeaking like crazy, scaring her half to death.

Then The Smallest Dog Ever distracted Jake and the other dogs while Lily escaped through a hole in the fence and out into an open field. Lily looked around for The Smallest Dog Ever but couldn't find him, which worried Lily until, without a peep, he arrived safe and sound right behind her, his short white fur barely ruffled.

Suddenly, it squeaked its name: Mortimer, which prompted Lily, in her most distinguished voice, to bark back, questioning his use of squeaks instead of barks for communication, Lily of the opinion that barks were much better.

They played hide and seek, each taking turns hiding between the hay bales, until, both exhausted, they fell asleep, curled up together on a hay bale under a slice of moon.

The next morning, before Jake and the other dogs awakened, Mortimer sneaked back into Jake's pen and stuffed dog food into his ample cheeks and spit them back out for Lily to eat.

Now, with her belly full, Lily was strong and ready to face The Big Noisy Things.

Running fast and furious they were, blowing their terrible black breath behind them in puffs of choking smoke that burned Lily's throat and eyes. She remembered The Man with The Hole in His Smile and how he had scooped up Lily and tossed her into that dark place where she had to defend herself against The Big Black Dog.

Lily turned and looked behind her, hoping to see The Lady with Sad Eyes, but she was nowhere in sight. Instead, Mortimer, The Smallest Dog Ever, squeaked that crazy language as he stood on the side of the highway, trying to persuade Lily to come back, though Lily was uncertain of what he really wanted, she largely unversed in squeak.

Fearlessly, she barked at The Big Noisy Things whizzing past her, their bad breath blowing her long hair this way and that. She remembered that Fredo was always unafraid, often returning in one of The Big Noisy Things and sometimes even chasing them down.

Then suddenly, one of The Big Noisy Things stopped right in front Lily. But Lily wasn't afraid. She stood her ground and wagged her tufted tail, newly fluffed by Mortimer. The Woman with Sad Eyes would get out of The Big Noisy Thing and scoop Lily up in her arms and take her away. But out from the Big Noisy Thing stepped another: a someone with big shiny eyes.

Before she could stop herself, Lily felt her body running across the asphalt as fast as her little legs would go. She leapt into the arms of The Shiny-Eyed, who carried the little dog into the belly of The Big Noisy Thing. Lily hoped it had been fed.

Lily jumped up on the seat and looked out of the car window at Mortimer, who was still on the side of the highway, pacing back and forth, his little whiskers twitching. Lily sadly barked good-bye, but Mortimer couldn't hear her over The Big Noisy Thing.

The Shiny-Eyed told Lily to lie down and behave, which Lily proceeded to do. But Lily couldn't wait to see The Lady with Sad Eyes or The Man with Kind Eyes. This Shiny-Eyed was a little scary.

Morgan-Chapter 11

Morgan's first thought, when she awoke, was that this day and every day forward would be Lily-less. She made herself open her eyes, their crystal blue only to be blinded by the morning sun pushing through the window sheers, forcing life into the bedroom. She must have slept late. The dogs were barking outside. She needed to get up to feed them.

But instead Morgan just lay there in the big old oak bed that she had slept in for almost all of her fifty-five years. Her small body was framed by seven sleeping dogs: one on its back, one on its belly, two under the covers, and three scattered around the bed like furry leaves.

Morgan heard a snore and rolled over to nudge Ray, who, apparently, had overslept, too. But it was Buster, not Ray, who was snoring and spooning Morgan like a lover. Morgan laughed and pushed Buster's massive paw from her shoulder. She raised herself up on her arm and leaned away from Buster's flat nose, mucus flying from it in fits and starts. She petted his soft head. His ill-constructed, human-engineered nose partially obstructed the boxer's airway, manifesting in the dog's forever, forlorn attempts to draw a bit of air into his lungs. The poor dog was snorting all night and day, awake or asleep, a slathering of snot in his wake.

Morgan had allowed Buster to sleep with her in the bed last night because the boxer had been sad, missing Lily. Usually, since Buster was so noisy and snotty, he slept on the floor beside Morgan's bed. Buster had been so happy about being in bed that he had licked Morgan to sleep.

Morgan had just started wondering where Ray was when he, still dressed in his red scrub shirt and jeans from the day before, trudged through the bedroom door.

"'Where have *you* been?" Morgan asked, sitting up, running her fingers through her short silver hair.

Ray, shaking his bald head, looked at Morgan as if she'd lost her mind. "I've been looking for Lily, of course. Where do you think I was? Out at a bar downing a few drinks, having a good time for a change?"

Morgan was in no mood. After all, it was Ray's fault that Lily got out. He was the one who had left the window, minus the screen he was mending, open in the bathroom. But she was the one who had left Lily in the bathroom. Morgan admitted to herself that she should have shut the open window.

"All night long, honey?" Morgan asked, trying to sound genuinely concerned.

"Yep." Ray plopped down in the chair by the bed and began taking off his muddy tennis shoes, their newness worn off after only a few dog days.

"Any luck?"

"Nope. But I did find her collar. It was by Jake's pen." Ray pulled Lily's powder-blue collar out of his pocket and handed it to Morgan.

"That's bad news," Morgan said, taking the collar. "I had just put her ID on there. I microchipped her, though. That's good." Morgan looked at the collar and noticed a deep scratch in the leather and the pink Y rhinestone missing. "She must have crawled under the fence or, hell, through the fence. Or over a fence. I better go see if there's a hole or something in it. You found it at Jake's fence, right?"

"Yep."

"Did you look to see if there was a hole?"

"Yeah, but I couldn't find anything," Ray said, his clothes still on him, climbing into bed.

"What are you doing?" Morgan jumped up, pulling the comforter off Ray. Buster woke and started snorting.

"I'm tired is what I am," Ray said, wiping off Buster's snot and rubbing it into Morgan's pillowcase for meanness.

Morgan punched him lightly in his arm. "No, you're helping me. You're not going to sleep."

She might find Lily. Or Lily might wander home. Someone might find the little Chinese-Crested and bring her back. The possibilities were limitless.

Ray and Morgan had spent a great deal of the previous night looking for Lily under the silver light of a quarter moon. Morgan had yelled and yelled for Lily until her voice was hoarse. With the help of a flashlight, she had looked around the yard and in the pasture. She had emailed the local sheriff's department, who would probably be no help, along with the local shelters. She had also put a missing dog alert on the McAfee Mutts website and Facebook, as well as listed Lily in a lost-dog on-line database.

"She couldn't get far, " Ray said, pushing himself back out of the bed.

"No, Ray," Morgan said, racing into the bathroom to wash her face. "Lily could get *very far, very fast*," she yelled. "Especially, if she's got something on her mind. Lily's not even spade."

"Oh, *no*," Ray said, a hint of sarcasm in his voice.

"Oh, *yes*," Morgan replied, trotting back into the bedroom, dabbing her face with a towel, trying hard not to respond to his thoughtless tone. She grabbed her overalls, which were already by the bed, where she'd laid them the night before. Morgan pulled them over her thin summer pajamas. "You were supposed to get it done today at the Fortville spay/neuter place. Too late for that now."

Ray tried to embrace Morgan, but she pushed him away and continued to buckle up her overalls.

"Morgan, we will find her," Ray said, giving up on anything more intimate and kissing her cheek instead. "Even if we don't, she'll be okay."

Morgan motioned toward the north window. "Ray, we've got a busy highway right out here. Did you check there?"

"Yep. I didn't find anything," Ray said, shaking his head, trying to pull off his clothes while standing but teetering instead, one pant leg on and one off.

"Good. Did you check the pasture again? You know we've got hungry coyotes. And big horses. Who could step on her. Or eat her. The coyotes, I mean."

"Yep, I saw nothing out there, either. Morgan, why are you worrying so much? We've done all we can for now. Besides, we've got plenty of dogs. We don't need anymore."

"Are you sure you fixed that fence that the car crashed through?"

"Of course, I fixed that fence. Those dogs would be out if I didn't, Morgan. They'd all be back out in the highway."

Morgan shook her head and stormed out of the room, stuffing Lily's collar into her pocket. She whistled for her dogs, who all perked their ears up, then lined up behind Morgan like *The Sound of Music's* vonTrapp family,

"Morgan, wait, I'm sorry. I'm coming," Ray yelled, losing his balance and falling back into bed. He quickly fell asleep before Morgan could respond, both arms above his head.

At least today the dental office was closed and the McAfees had the day off. But Morgan didn't know where to begin. She had already slept late by a couple of hours because she'd forgotten to set her alarm last night. But in the hallway were seven furry, eager faces, seven wagging tails behind them, all waiting to do their business. Other dogs to deal with were right outside, too. Morgan could hear most of them barking.

Surely, if someone found Lily, they would trace her microchip.

Every time her time cell phone rang, Morgan answered it, hoping it was someone who had found Lily. But it was always someone who had found another dog or lost a dog or saw a starving dog or saw a hot dog or saw a waterless dog or saw a scared dog or just saw a dog. Morgan, who usually knew what to do, suddenly didn't know what to do, as if she'd lost the script in her brain that she had always referred to after dealing with years and years of endless dog scenarios. She told them to call the dogcatcher or take the dog to the shelter, giving them the address, knowing it was Wednesday, Derril's day to volunteer at the shelter. Derril spent most of the day there when it was his day to volunteer. Derril hadn't much else to do. He was retired with few hobbies or relationships, other than his mother. Morgan called Derril to see if the dogcatcher had possibly found Lily and had tossed her back into the kennel with the doberman.

"Lily ran away? That's awful," Derril yelled over the deafening dog din at the shelter. "You say you lost Lily? That's a shame. But we need bleach," said Derril, changing the subject. "And that toothless dogcatcher did bring in a whole litter of red tick hound pups. They look pretty good. Not sick."

Morgan knew Derril followed good parvovirus protocol but felt she needed to remind him anyway. Too many pups had died. "Just make sure you use good parvo procedures, Derril," Morgan said, knowing that Derril was very careful, but she didn't want to take any chances. "And make sure you mop their kennel first with fresh bleach water. And don't move the pups. They have to stay in the kennels so as not to transmit parvo."

"What did you say?" Derril screamed then totally changed the subject again, unaware of what the subject was. "Hey, I'm supposed to know if I got on that Fortville animal board soon."

Morgan didn't want to talk to Derril, who was difficult to get off the phone with. Now he couldn't even hear what she was saying, making for a longer, even more unsuccessful conversation. "I am so excited for you, Derril," Morgan said, trying to be happy for him. But Morgan had Lily on her mind.

It was a long shot, but Morgan would drive into Multown and ask around to see if anyone had seen Lily. Lily could be trying to get back into town. After all, the dogcatcher found her there, and Lily was in the shelter there for a few hours.

As she fed the outside dogs at her house, Morgan tried to remember any clues that might help her locate Lily. She remembered the dogcatcher had said he had found Lily on Highway 64, which ran through the middle of Multown and was a strange place to find a dog like Lily with a fancy collar--in an area with lower-income households. It was likely that Lily had been dumped there, but it was still so weird. Who would dump an expensive dog like that?

Morgan spent the rest of the afternoon going door-to-door in downtown Multown seeing if anyone had seen a black-and-white polka-dotted, furless dog with tufts of strange hair all over it. She didn't have a photo of Lily, so she found a photo on the Internet, printed it and took it with her.

Most of the Multown residents thought she was silly for wanting a crazy, useless dog like that but said if they did see it, they would give her a call. Many of them kindly proffered up one or two or three of their dogs since she needed one so badly.

"That spotted bitch there might be pregnant," said an old lady in a crop top with *Foxy* emblazoned across it. She pointed at a puny Australian shepherd lying on her front porch. "Now *that's* a great deal. You can have them all." Morgan guessed she would be getting them all eventually anyway.

She had just about given up looking for Lily when she stopped at the old Quickie Mart to get herself a Coke. She was thirsty, the sun relentless. She had talked to so many people that her throat, already hoarse from yelling so much last night for Lily, had started hurting.

The store was ancient, a lean-to bait shop in the back of it, an old self-serve icebox full of bottle Cokes in the corner. Growing up, Morgan had spent a lot of time there. She had even bought beer here for her daddy who would sit out in his old truck and wait for the little girl in the overalls to bring out a six-pack. His friend, Roger, the old Choctaw store owner, had sold beer to Morgan since she was old enough to walk. Morgan climbed out of the van and went into the store. The old-fashioned store bells on a leather string jingled behind her when she closed the door.

"Hey, Morgan," Roger said, grinning at her with new teeth the Choctaw government had just made for him. "What's you been up to?"

"Just need a Coke," Morgan smiled, stopping in front of the counter, long tall Roger slumped over it. Morgan waved toward the window facing the parking lot, the heat radiating off it making ghosts. "Hot out there."

"What brings you to town today? Thought today was your day off." Roger knew this because his store was right across from Morgan and Ray's dental office.

Plus, the old Choctaw was nosy. Roger knew everything that went on in Multown, although that wasn't much.

"It is," Morgan said, "but I'm in town looking for a dog."

"You're looking for a dog? I figure you're the last person in the world who needs another dog. I'd say you got plenty of them. Whatcha doin' that for?"

Morgan pulled the photo from her bib pocket and showed it to Roger. "This is the dog I'm looking for, Roger," Morgan said. "It's called a Chinese-Crested. Black spots on pinkish, almost hairless skin with tufts of long white hair all over its body. On it's points. Its head. Its tail. Its feet."

Roger took the photo in his long fingers, brown from Choctaw blood and nicotine. "What's wrong with that dog? It got mange? It don't have any hair. Ever bathe them in old motor oil? Great to get rid of mange."

Morgan retrieved the photo. "Yes, but Roger, it probably wouldn't be that great for the dog. Lord, it could kill them."

"Could kill this one you're looking for she's so puny. Oh, well, what's that they say? Two birds with one stone?"

Roger loved to jest with Morgan, but she wasn't in the mood today. Roger made no bones about shooting an animal if he thought it needed to be shot. Most people in the area were of like mind.

Morgan walked to the back of the store where the bait shop was and peered into the minnow well. Inside a few slivers of silver, still alive, caught the light, but most of the silver, motionless, floated on the top. Pushing back the lid of the old refrigerated Coke box, again she remembered her father. She grabbed a bottle of Coke and pressed it against her forehead for a moment, the cool, hopefully, making its way to her soul. She walked back to the convenience store and placed her Coke on the counter, setting it next to the energy supplements and electronic cigarettes.

"Roger, anyway, have you seen that dog? Her name is Lily."

Roger grinned, his white teeth gleaming. He tossed back his bushy black head as if he had just heard the best joke ever, his casino ball cap falling off his head. "Guess what? I have seen that dog. What're the odds?"

Morgan tried not to get too excited but couldn't help it and grabbed his tattooed arm. "Oh my gosh, when?"

Roger put her Coke in a plastic sack. "A couple a days ago. I think it jumped out of a van window while this person was in here paying for some gas. I didn't see that happen but..."

"Really?"

"Woman got out of the car and tried to chase it. I thought she got it. But I guess not."

"I guess not. Don't guess you've got anything on her."

"Nope. White van. Old VW van. I remember Arkansas plates. That's all we know. She paid with cash. She only got ten bucks worth of gas, I think."

"That's so strange. It looks like she would've looked longer if it was her own dog."

"I guess. But the world's a strange place. Nothing makes sense anymore. What else can I do for you?"

Morgan took her sack and gathered it to her. "Do you remember the license plate number?"

"No, but I do remember a bumper sticker."

"What did it say?"

"I love China Chests. Had a heart and one of these dogs like in your picture." Roger bent over and picked up his hat, dusted it off on his knee and placed it back on top of his bushy head of salt-and-pepper hair.

"Weird. Something like that. I mean, why would you like Chinese chests? Those women are small-breasted, ain't they?"

"That's it?"

Roger scrunched up his brown eyes, furrowing his dark, smooth forehead, Morgan wondering if the old man had sold his soul to the devil for ageless skin. "Oh, the woman was tall and skinny, nice-looking lady with these green eyes that sort of made her look like a reptile, wide set eyes, sort of almost on the side of her head. I hear that happens to kids when their parents drink. Something called fatal alcohol syndrome. Shame, ain't it? I got a cousin that happened to."

Morgan stopped by the Piggly Wiggly to pick up several bottles of bleach and drove to the shelter, which was a full house again no matter how hard Morgan tried to get the dogs fostered or adopted. On her way to the laundry room, she stopped and looked at the new hound puppies wriggling around on the cement floor of a kennel. Their mama, emaciated, but still letting her babies suck, had bug brown eyes sunk in their sockets with grim glimmers of hope still lingering. Morgan didn't know what she was going to do with them but couldn't think about it now.

In the next kennel was the abandoned collie mix that had been left at the dental office. The collie mix was in better spirits, not as squeamish, and was sharing a tug with a husky-corgi with big ears, blue eyes and very short legs.

Morgan walked on to the laundry room, trying not to look at anymore dogs as she went by, knowing they were just fine, that Derril had taken care of them, although Morgan could never imagine someone, other than herself, taking better care of the dogs.

She figured Derril would be gone, but he was still there, folding what he called "poopie towels," which he would later stack neatly into a bin sitting by the washer and dryer. Derril sat cross-legged style on the floor in the laundry room, his hairy legs sporting knee-length bermuda shorts that he'd probably owned since 1972. He reminded Morgan of an old boy scout.

"Derril, what are you still doing here?" Morgan asked, spooking him so that Derril dropped the towel.

Derril, grimacing a bit, picked up the towel and started folding again. "Folding poopie towels. What are you doing? It's your day off."

Morgan crossed her arms across her bibbed chest. "Derril, I called you at ten this morning. You've been here for six hours."

"I know, but that's okay. I think the dogs appreciate their towels folded."

"I don't think they care."

"That's not what Mouse said," Derril said, looking up, smiling like an ancient Dudley Do-Right.

Mouse was a little Pekingese in the shelter that Derril had taken a liking to, but his mother had said no when Derril asked if he could foster her.

"I bet Lily will be back before you know it," said Derril, always the optimist no matter how many dogs he had to clean up after.

"Thank you for helping the homeless animals, Derril," Morgan said, turning and heading down the hallway toward the exit door. "See you at your meeting next Thursday. You'll do great on that animal board in Fortville."

Derril poked his head into the hallway. "Morgan?"

Morgan turned around.

Derril looked as if he might cry. "Where's the old white schnauzer, Buddy? I didn't see him today."

Morgan turned around and kept walking, tossing the words behind her, trying to lose them. "I took him home. He'll be much happier there. He's just getting too old to adopt to anyone."

Beatrice- Chapter 12

Beatrice, sitting by herself at a folding table in a windowless lunchroom at Computerville, was on her lunch break. The only other sign of life, besides Beatrice, who was fast waning in that classification since Martina's death, was a computer-generated flier hanging by the microwave that was soliciting employees for softball team. Beatrice and Dotty, who wasn't even a Computerville employee, were the only people signed up to play. Despite high hopes for a team, never enough people were interested, yet the sign hung year after year.

"But why do you think he won't answer my calls?" asked Beatrice on her cell phone with Al Nosack's receptionist on the other end.

"I am not sure, Miss..."

"*Cooper*," Beatrice shot back. "Please make sure he calls me," she barked, trying her best to be firm, yet not too crazy, though crazy was right around the corner. "I must talk to him. Today."

"Yes, Miss um.."

"*Cooper,*" Beatrice yelled before she could stop herself. She jerked the phone up in the air as if that would stop her very loud voice from making its way through the airwaves to the receptionist.

Beatrice tried again to compose herself, unsure why she was getting so upset and soothed her voice. "I'm sorry. I just must speak to him."

"Yes, Cooper, I will. Not to worry."

"It's not *Cooper*, it's *Beatrice*," Beatrice said, spitting out the words, visualizing them nailed around the receptionist's head. "*Beatrice Cooper*. Oh, never mind."

Beatrice ended the call without saying good-bye, which was indeed bad form but in no way compared with Nosack's lack of manners.

Why wouldn't Nosack call her back? She had called him twice that morning and written him an email explaining the reasons why Derril Harmon wasn't qualified to be on Beatrice's animal board.

Beatrice, after all, had done some vetting.

Derril Harmon, who still lived with his mother in Fortville, for crying out loud, volunteered for an animal shelter in *Multown, Oklahoma*, not *Fortville, Arkansas*. The position specified that the applicant needed to be a board member of a non-profit animal welfare organization comprised primarily of *Fortville residents*. Beatrice had found out that McAfee's Mutts, located in Multown, Oklahoma, was made up of volunteers who, for the most part, were *Oklahoma* residents. To make matters worse, a crazy woman named Morgan McAfee ran that shelter. Beatrice knew about that Morgan McAfee and the way she believed, always making trouble. McAfee was a member of PETA and had protested circuses and circulated petitions making animal cruelty a felony in both Oklahoma and Arkansas. Her behavior was reckless. Her kind wasn't needed. And Morgan McAfee and Lance Blackmon were friends, practically in cahoots. All of those people who rescued dogs were in favor of this spay/neuter ordinance. Blackmon had even given that silly McAfee some sort of humanitarian award that was covered in the local paper.

But Beatrice was running out of time. Tomorrow, at a noon study session, the City Council would vote on Harmon's application. She had to convince someone that Harmon was unqualified or he would be approved for membership on the animal board. And that would be the end of her vow to get rid of the proposed spay/neuter ordinance.

Beatrice looked at her belly bulging over her *I Love Italian Greyhounds* belt buckle, the "s" at the end of *Greyhounds* the only letter visible.

Beatrice, stress-eating since Martina's death and all these crazy animal politics, was spending too much time at Taco Bell. For the past two weeks, every weeknight, from five to ten, Beatrice would order hourly, in ten-dollar increments, from the dollar menu, which had resulted in the already big Beatrice growing even bigger.

Beatrice, wishing for a window if only to gaze upon a dead bug or a colorful parking space, stared at the stark white walls of the lunchroom. She grabbed her lunch sack out of her satchel and placed it on the table then opened it and scarfed down her chicken breast in three big bites. Her potato chips were next, which she polished off in four bites. She gulped her apple down in five bites.

Beatrice, a food separatist, tolerated no food group integration. The only exception was Taco Bell five-layer burritos and chalupas. She even consumed her food in a certain order: first the entree, then the sides (from lightest to darkest), next bread and, finally, dessert.

In addition to all these food rules, Beatrice ate very fast, there never enough grub to be got growing up with a large mother and a very big brother. Plus, Big Berta had to scrape by a living for her family with no husband to help out. So the Coopers, who grew up on the poor side of Fortville, had survived on what Big Berta's mother had fed her in the Cookson Hills of Oklahoma where she was raised: boiled hog jowl, fried mush, free polk salet (if one got there before the city mowed) and turnip greens. As a kid, Beatrice would also sneak Purina Dog Chow, a good and tasty filler.

(Even now, Beatrice had to quell her hankering for it when passing by the dog food in the grocery store.)

Beatrice crumpled up her lunch sack and tossed it back in her satchel. Maybe she could eat Derril Harmon. That would solve her problems.

If his application was approved, he would cause a fuss on the animal board and ruin all Beatrice's plans. He was for mandatory spay/neuter, she knew that. They were all for it at that McAfee Mutts. He might sway people on the new animal board toward thinking that way. But the mandatory spay/neuter ordinance was never going to pass, no matter how long they tabled it. It just gave Beatrice more time to fight it. And blog about it. And kill it. *Or euthanize it.* Beatrice pulled out her cell phone and called Dotty.

"Hello?" said Dotty's nasal voice, a little more anxious than usual.

"What are you doing?" Beatrice asked, trying to sound nonchalant, as if a freight train wasn't running over her and Beatrice tied to the rails.

"I'm out on the street feeding homeless people," Dotty answered, sarcastic yet bubbly somehow. "What do you think I'm doing?"

"Have you got a second?"

"Not really," Dotty replied.

Beatrice heard a tussle of some sort then a muffled, "Hey, give me my phone back."

"Hello? Hello?" Beatrice asked, unsure if Dotty was still on the other end. "Dotty, are you there?"

Beatrice heard a few hollow thwacks followed by a long pause of dead silence. Finally, Dotty returned to the phone. "Hello, Beatrice?"

"Yes, Dotty, I'm here," Beatrice replied.

"What's up?" Dotty said, a little out of breath. "I just had to take care of some business there. Just a homeless guy I had to hit. Sorry."

"Al Nosack won't call me back." Beatrice had to swallow hard to keep the tears from coming. She had been crying a lot lately, which was unusual for the unemotional Beatrice.

"Are you kidding? That's crazy. Who does he think he is?" Dotty asked sullenly, her effervescence suddenly fizzled out.

"I don't know. The city administrator, maybe. Could you call him for me?" Beatrice took her crumpled sack from her satchel and wiped her nose with it.

"Bea, I can't. The Homeless Angels are up for non-profit awards and we need the money the city allocates to us."

"So, you can't help me?"

"No, I can't. It just too great a risk to make the city mad at me right now."

"Then can you apply for the animal board, please? You'd be perfect for it."

"Bea, I don't have the time. I'm going crazy as it is. My new crocheting class is taking up a lot of time." Dotty had turned over a new leaf and was starting some new hobbies.

"So what can I do?" Beatrice asked, desperate. "I've called and e-mailed him, and he won't return any of them."

"Heck, Beatrice, go to his office. Confront him. He just works downtown at the city offices. Do it."

When she was in the Fortville Citizens Academy, Beatrice had toured the city offices, which were in an old building downtown that had once been a grand bank. It was like so many graceful old structures that had been forced to keep up with the times, like an old man in a wheelchair wearing a gold leisure suit, a gold chain draped around his neck and a pimp daddy fedora atop his head. Where once high fresco and tin ceilings had been, there were now lowered popcorn ones with fluorescent lights. Veneer wood paneling spread upon the walls like a brown disease.

Beatrice exhaled slowly, watching her big belly eclipse the "s" in *Greyhounds* on her belt buckle. "Okay, I"ll do that."

"Good for you. Be a big girl."

I am already a big girl, Beatrice thought as she pressed the End button on her phone and tucked it inside her satchel. Beatrice got up and tossed her satchel over her shoulder, trudged into the bathroom, closed the door of the stall and slammed down the toilet lid. She folded her long body down, her knees touching the door. From her satchel, she removed the crumpled paper sack, opened it and dumped its contents on the floor. Then she placed the mouth of the sack over her own. When Beatrice screamed into the sack, no one heard her, not even Beatrice.

A few moments later, Beatrice was back to writing computer programs for the logistics of a local factory. She emailed her boss asking for permission to leave work early. He immediately emailed back permission, although she had taken a personal day the day before to go to the Tulsa Dog Show. Beatrice was a good employee and had perfect attendance for fifteen years, not logging a single sick day since she had joined Computerville right of college.

As Beatrice was driving down the wide swath of Post Avenue in downtown Fortville, she imagined what it was like in its heyday. Beatrice was too young to remember any color in the old black-and-white town. Big Berta had told Beatrice that a photographer, like a paparazzo, would snap photos of the downtown shoppers, dressed top to toe in their very finest clothes, carrying their pretty packages as if they were prized possessions.

Beatrice passed by the ancient courthouse and the hanging gallows, built in the mid- and late-eighteen hundreds, respectively, on the city's far northwestern edge. These were enduring relics of the past from which the city of Fortville had tumbled. Now a boring national historic site, the two-story red brick building and its white-washed wooden gallows tamely guarded the Oklahoma frontier to the west, where the former Indian Territory's teepees had morphed into casinos and prohibition whiskey had become crystal meth.

Beatrice circled the block several times until a parking spot came open, pulled in and shut off the engine. She carefully opened her door after the traffic had gone by, got out, closed the door and scurried, as much as Beatrice could scurry, to the parking meter, where a homeless man had decided to make his new home. After fending off the homeless man's pleas for her meter money and feeding the meter instead, Beatrice headed into the dull-cream-colored, ten-story building.

Beatrice studied the building directory, a black-slotted board with movable white letters hanging beside an old brass elevator. She thought the sign had probably been there since 1939, only the names changing. Nosack's office was on the third floor.

Beatrice took the stairs, the old elevator too confining, and plodded up them until her left sandal fell off, prompting her to remove her right sandal and scaled, sock-footed, the second flight. Out of breath by the time she got to the third-floor landing, she plopped down on the step and dusted off her socks and jammed her sandals back on her big feet. She pulled herself up and walked through the door.

Suddenly, Beatrice froze mid-lurch, a Birkenstock sandal dangling from her tube-socked foot, Beatrice resembling a very large short-haired pointer.

The pretty receptionist had curly red hair like an Irish Setter and brown eyes that one could drown in. Even with a big inner tube. And a life jacket. "Miss Cooper?" The young girl asked, looking up at Beatrice, catching Beatrice staring at her.

"Oh, yes, that's me," Beatrice fumbled and looked down.

"Mr. Nosack said to have you sent in as soon as you got here," said the receptionist, still so young she had braces on her teeth.

"Really?" Beatrice checked herself and wondered if she was still in the same universe as she was this morning when Nosack wouldn't acknowledge her existence.

"He did," said the receptionist.

"Hey, Beatrice," Al Nosack said, walking out his office. "How are you doing?"

Al looked more pinched and red-faced than usual. At least he was faking a smile. Beatrice walked toward him, extending her big hand, dwarfing Nosack's small delicate one. He shook Beatrice's hand. "Fine, Al, and you?"

Nosack turned and walked back into his office, motioning for Beatrice to follow. "I'm good. I understand you want to talk. Let's do it."

"Okay."

Beatrice, a bit dazed, walked into Nosack's office only to be greeted by the many heads of dead animals mounted on his dark-paneled walls. A sad, sinking feeling, only exacerbated by the very low, very small olive-green chair that she soon sat down in, plunged through her.

Nosack looked at his land-line phone, the call buttons darkened, and frowned. "Well, Beatrice, what is it exactly that you wanted to talk to me about? Jennifer said it was urgent that you see me."

Beatrice tried to look at him but couldn't, so she concentrated on the stuffed pheasant to Nosack's right. "I sent emails and tried to call you..."

"Yes, I know but haven't had time to tend to them," Nosack replied. "I guess you can tell me now what you want. You are certainly persistent. I will give you that."

"I needed to talk about Derril Harmon and his application for the animal board." There, she said it. It wasn't like Nosack didn't know this already.

Nosack played with his pen, a really nice one, Beatrice wondering what one did with a pen these days.

"What is you want to know?" Nosack asked.

The old play dumb trick wasn't going to work on her. "We wrote," Beatrice began, "in the ordinance that was passed by the city that two people needed to be on the board of a non-profit animal welfare organization to be on our new animal board." Beatrice kept her eyes on the pheasant's beady ones, hoping it would bolster her courage. "And that the organization's membership must be comprised of primarily residents of *Fortville*. This Harmon volunteers for McAfee Mutts in *Multown*. In other words, he isn't eligible."

"But another ordinance we have in Fortville overrides your stipulation."

"What ordinance is that?" Beatrice asked, her face with an expression not unlike the one on the stuffed deer head.

Nosack pulled a big book out of the bookshelf behind him and slammed it on the top of his desk.

"Section 103-11 which amends Section 2-48 of the Fortville Municipal Code and requires the City Council appoint only registered voters of the city of Fortville to boards and commissions. It seemed redundant to include language that was already in place in the form of an ordinance."

Beatrice paused for a moment, searching for another dead animal to look at but found none and looked back at Nosack. "But that is not the same," Beatrice stammered.

"Derril Harmon is a registered voter of Fortville. That's the only requirement that needs to be fulfilled," Nosack countered. "It's not necessary that the board he is on represents an animal welfare organization comprised mostly of *Fortville* residents."

"But I don't think he's even a board member."

"His application states he is."

"Well, that's not what it says on the McAfee Mutts website. It says he's only a foster and a volunteer." Beatrice fumbled in her satchel for her laptop. "Here, let me show you."

Nosack put up his tiny hand like he was trying to direct traffic, albeit very small traffic. "Beatrice, we have made sure he is on the board at McAfee Mutts. Derril

Harmon is an eligible candidate for the animal board. I'm sorry."

Beatrice looked again at the dead heads on his wall. "But those people over there at that Multown shelter are are crazy, I've heard. They don't even like real dogs."

"Real dogs?"

"Purebred dogs with papers. They're against the American Dog Club, too." Beatrice looked around the room for some sign of a hunting dog photo, Nosak surely with enough dead stuff on his walls to warrant one. "What kind of dog do you have, Al?"

"An English setter and a black lab."

Beatrice smiled through her shiny teeth. "So, you have purebreds?"

"Yes, I do," Nosack said, nodding his thick head of slicked-back hair, not a single hair out of place. "But I have one other dog."

Beatrice leaned forward, her knees touching his desk. "Oh, yeah, what kind is that?"

"A Heinz 57 from the Fortville shelter."

"Oh, that's good. Nice thing to do." Beatrice tucked her chin down, got up and walked out of the door without looking back. She did, however, sneak a glance at the pretty receptionist.

Fall

Lily - Chapter 13

The leaves had fallen like Lily's heart.

The little dog tried to wrap her tail around her to stop the shivering, but the Chinese-Crested's skinny tail, as lovely as it was, was no help, the shivering turning to shaking.

So she tried to sleep and forget.

But as she balanced on the thin, rusty chicken wire, the floor of her new home, turning her little body round in circles to try to lie down, one of her paws slipped, slicing her foot. Sad and bleeding, Lily sat on her haunches, licking her paw, until she saw the slice of moon in the dark sky. The moon reminded her of

Mortimer, The Smallest Dog Ever, when they had played hide and seek amongst the hay bales at the house of The Lady with Sad Eyes.

Suddenly, Lily bristled at the scent of The Shiny-Eyed and heard the slamming noise that sometimes brought food. The Big Noisy Thing bellowed, which meant The Shiny-Eyed was playing with The Big Noisy Thing instead of feeding Lily. Sometimes that happened.

The little Chinese-Crested, who had grown a big belly despite having nothing in it, watched as The Big Noisy Thing tried to catch the slice of moon, running closer and closer to it.

I bet I could catch that slice of moon, Lily thought, unafraid.

Lily felt a rough wetness on her neck and turned to see Sam, her new friend, and returned his gesture with a lick of her own. Lily certainly needed a bath and grooming, Sam good for both. He would keep Lily warm on a cold night as this.

The two, wound round one another, slept most of the night, until the other crying boxes woke them.

But before that Lily dreamed about The Man with Kind Eyes who took Lily to places with other dogs who would do tricks while eyes of all kinds watched. The Lady with Mean Eyes went, too, but sometimes she would take Lily to places all by herself.

Morgan-Chapter 14

Because Jake, the bulldog, was receiving visitors today, Morgan was bathing him. He wasn't the most perceptive of Morgan's dogs; however, he knew something was different, Jake livelier than his usual apathetic bulldog self.

Standing in the aluminum wash tub with soapy water up to his massive, wrinkled neck, Jake licked Morgan five very wet times, smudging her make-up, something Morgan rarely donned. But on adoption days, the woman, who normally didn't give a damn what people thought, wanted to make a good impression, which resulted in Morgan dolling herself up, as Ray called it.

Morgan laughed, wiped her face and continued scrubbing the brown, soon-to-be-white-again English bulldog. She lifted up his folds of skin and washed in between them, not knowing what she might find. She had rescued a cocker spaniel from the Fortville stockyards with an infected ear. Maggots had buried into it and eaten the flesh. A portion of his ear, so rotten and festered, had had to be amputated. But Jake was fine, folds and all.

"Aw, Jake, you're feeling good. Aren't you, buddy? That's good," Morgan said, scratching him between his ears. "Some people are coming to visit you today, Jakie." Morgan poured a pan of warm rinse water over him, careful to keep it out of his eyes. "You had better be on your best behavior."

Morgan didn't dare tell the dogs what could happen that day. That someone might want them. That someone might, in fact, love them. Morgan didn't want to get up their hopes or disappoint them if they didn't get picked. But by this stage of a potential adoption at McAfee Mutts, that hardly ever happened.

When potential parents arrived, usually they had already developed a bond with the dog. Morgan had learned the hard way by losing an adopted-out dog through a faulty fence. Only perfect homes (and yes, there were perfect homes) were fit for a McAfee Mutt. Morgan personally made visits to the applicants' homes to check out the living conditions as well as vetted them by checking peer and vet references. She also sent them beautiful digital photos of the dogs along with a whole lot of persuasion specially manufactured by the uncompromising Morgan McAfee. Before the potential adopter reached the shelter, they were ready to sign the papers and take the dog home, excited about their new family member despite the dogs' flaws, some with quite a few. It was an honor to be a human member of the McAfee Mutt pack.

Jake shook off the water and paraded around the concrete paddock on his short bowed legs, causing a big ruckus. He was a dog out of order and not in his pen while the other dogs, most all seventy-four or so, looked him over, barking. Jake loved the attention.

Morgan tied a newly donated skull-and-cross bones neckerchief around Jake's neck and clasped a sturdy leash on Jake's collar. Jake fought the leash so hard that Morgan had to turn and drag him under the shade of the old maple tree and clasp his leash on a ring embedded in the tree. Ray had drilled a ring into the old tree's trunk despite his protestations, the tree a gift from Ray to Morgan on their first wedding anniversary. But the tree had been all right, bursting burnt-orange every autumn for more than three decades. It was a yearly reminder of the McAfee's love for one other and, more importantly, as Morgan often reminded Ray, how wrong he had been about piercing the tree, he so worried that the ring screw might kill it.

Jake's "maybes" (potential adopters) were coming all the way from Fort Worth, Texas. Morgan, though always nervous when someone came to see one of her dogs, was excited because these visits were what made all the dogs' deaths, all the disease and hurt, and, lately, all the local politics, worthwhile. Everything she did was for this moment.

Jake would have surely been dead if it hadn't been for Morgan, who had rescued him from a nearby puppy mill, which was just down Highway 64, only a few miles from their house.

Jake had a misshapen front right leg because he and his sibling, had, more than likely, been ill-bred. At puppy mills, the breeder would often breed siblings together or fathers with daughters or mothers with sons. This was not good for genetics in any dog, let alone purebred dogs, which were usually less hardy than the mixed-pedigree dogs that usually showed up at McAfee Mutts. But purebred dogs sometimes found their way to McAfee Mutts, too.

Morgan had found Jake and his sister, BeBe, in a tiny cage of rusty chicken wire raised a little off the ground by a couple of cement blocks. Inside were the two shriveled little bulldog pups, starving and cold, with only a piece of wet cardboard and two empty whipped topping bowls. The entire puppy mill was stinking to high heaven with dog feces piled just as high when a few moments past midnight on a Saturday night, Morgan had sneaked in to rescue the poor dogs. She heard the cock of a shotgun when she nabbed Jake and BeBe, quickly tucking them under her sweat shirt. She had raced to the van and dove into the passenger's seat as Ray stepped on the gas, Ray later saying he had hoped the old van still had some kick. Morgan was still working with PETA on evidence to shut down the puppy mill, a difficult feat to accomplish in even the best (meaning worst) circumstances.

Under the blazing burnt orange canopy of the McAfees' old maple, Jake passed gas then splayed himself out, kicking his hind legs behind him and laying his belly flat on the cool grass. He licked his misshapen front leg that instead of bowing out, bowed inward, forcing Jake to walk with a small limp. He ignored the other dogs that were checking him out until taking a sniff and going on their merry way again.

"Oh, God, please let your will be done, but I hope that your will is that the Claytons go home with Jake," Morgan whispered before planting a kiss on the rough, dry nose of Bart, the old sheepdog, one of the permanent residents of the coveted feed room. His long, curly hair had been matted in dreadlocks by Morgan's daughter, Paisley, who had come home on fall break. Bart would die at McAfee Mutts along with charter member, Lucky, the beagle, who, though the first dog to go up for adoption, still hadn't been adopted after seven years. But that didn't bother Lucky, who was taking a dip in his water trough after kicking out one of the young whippersnappers who didn't know the rules.

"Morgan, someone's at the gate, honking," Ray yelled, poking his bald, shiny head out of the kitchen door. "Probably the people from Fort Worth."

"Gee, Ray, you think?" Morgan thought, wondering why Ray was still in the house and not outside. "Come help me, Ray," Morgan said, motioning for him to come out. She always needed him for people handling if he didn't talk them to death first. At least he talked. Morgan was usually mute, looking down at the ground, stubbing the toes of her muck boots into the ground like she was putting out an invisible cigarette.

Ray hollered back, smiling like a Cheshier cat, Morgan none too happy about it. "Be out in a second, my love."

Morgan saw a nice SUV pulling into the driveway. She ran toward the gate, trying not to be excited, but her heart was bursting through her sweater, an old boucle one she had had since high school.

She waved at the people in the car then opened the heavy gate. Morgan motioned for them to pull through.

They had barely parked beside her old Mercedes before two children, a girl and a boy, with bright smiling faces and just as bright blonde hair on top of their heads, tumbled out from opposite sides of the SUV.

Next, two grown-ups, dressed in top-to-toe Eddie Bauer, came out of the car, both on their cell phones. Finally, out leaped a toy poodle, which caused quite a stir, the McAfee dogs already barking before, ratcheting up their performance a notch. All the outside dogs had been put up in their pens and the house dogs secured inside, so Morgan wasn't worried too much about the safety of the poodle. But she knew it would be best for the poodle to stay in the SUV, so Jake could calmly meet her in the presence of her guardians.

"Hey, welcome," Morgan said, upping her voice a notch, trying to speak above the barking din. Morgan bent to pet the poodle, who had already taken off in the direction of the barking dogs. The poodle pointed its perky nose up to the chain link fence, where Jake lay behind it. The poodle yapped as the pink bow on top of its head threatened to fall off at every bark.

"Hi, where's Jake?" said the young boy, dressed more Old Navy than Eddie Bauer.

Looking down the hill, Morgan pointed at Jake, who hadn't moved, his legs still kicked out from under him, the dog without a care in the world, not even barking, looking in no specific direction. His tongue, the only moving object, dangled from his shiny lips in self-absorbed-Jake fashion.

The Claytons had sent Morgan photos depicting the place where Jake might make his new home. They lived in a beautiful home that looked like a castle with little white rocks instead of grass for a yard. They had written that it was just too hot to maintain grass. A yard of white rocks probably wasn't the best yard for a dog, but she didn't think Jake would mind as long as it was enclosed with a good fence since bulldogs had a tendency to roam.

"Let's go see him, come on," Morgan said, motioning for the family to follow her. Through the chain-link fence, the little poodle was still yapping as Jake stood up. Morgan knew Jake got along with most of the dogs but wasn't sure about the poodle, especially one that he had just met. Morgan stopped and looked at the adults. "Do you think we could keep the poodle in the truck until you meet Jake first?" Morgan asked meekly. "I think that would be better."

The woman, Beth Clayton, looked a bit peeved, but followed Morgan's instructions with a nod of her pretty head. "Mia, go get Bitty and take her back to the truck, please."

Mia ran to get the yappy little dog, who was none too happy about it, while Jake, nonplussed, watched. The little boy was already through the gate before Morgan could tell him to wait, and there was Bitty, right on his heels, barely out of Mia's arms.

"Uh-oh," Morgan said, taking off down the hill with Beth running after Morgan and her husband, Rick, right behind them both. Morgan thought she heard the kitchen door slam and turned and yelled, still running, "Ray, come help us! Bring a leash."

But it was too late, the Jake/Bitty mash-up was already in progress. By the time the adults reached the dogs, the poodle was licking Jake and the little boy was petting Jake, who had jumped up, as much as Jake could jump and was licking the little boy.

"Looks like a lot of licking going on," said Rick, whose dog Jake would be if he could wrestle it away from his son now. Rick had grown up with English bulldogs but wanted to wait until his children were older to get one. Morgan knew this from Rick's application.

"How does he do on his leg that's not quite right?" asked Rick, pointing at Jake.

Morgan unhooked the leash from tree and let Jake roam to show how Jake could rock it, gimp leg and all.

"He does okay," said Morgan. "Go on Jake. Show them how you don't let that leg slow you down."

Bitty teased Jake, and Jake trotted after her, but it wasn't long before Jake, doing some extra heavy breathing, was lying on the grass again.

Rick pulled back Jake's flopping jaws and examined his teeth, then rubbed Jake's malformed leg, bending it back and forth. Jake didn't mind it a bit. The bulldog rolled over on his back, waving his four legs up in the air, showing submission to Rick, the ultimate compliment.

The meeting couldn't be going better until Morgan saw Bitty in the pasture. Bitty had somehow gotten through the fence, and Daisy was flaring her nostrils, her head down toward the ground, circling the poodle.

Suddenly, poodle Bitty became a piece of barking fluff flying through the air like a milkweed seed on an updraft.

"Oh my gosh," Morgan said, waving her hands up in the air.

"Oh, my goodness, Bitty!" Beth yelled, already navigating her way down the hill expertly in her high-heel boots, the dogs in pens barking at her along the way, like a Greek chorus. "My baby," Beth said, motioning toward her husband, who was far behind. "Rick, come on."

Daisy had kicked Bitty. And though Morgan had missed seeing the impact, she betted it had been a pretty tough blow. By the time Morgan got there, Beth had picked up Bitty, cradling her in her arms. The little poodle was shaken up but looked intact, except for its missing its bow, which Morgan found and handed to Mia.

"I'm so sorry," said Morgan, stubbing the ground with the toes of her muck boots.

Beth cooed over the poodle, who wasn't even bleeding. Morgan thought the dog looked a little cock-eyed but surmised the poodle had looked that way before meeting Daisy, though Morgan couldn't remember for sure.

"Here let me check her for broken bones," Morgan said, reaching for Bitty until the poodle snapped at her. "Damn," Morgan said before realizing what she had said and how it sounded, Morgan not much of a curser. "I'm sorry," she said, putting her hand over her mouth. "At least, let's take her to the vet. There's one right down the road. I'll pay for it."

Jake had come down for the party, too, even venturing a bark occasionally, and Rick had finally shown up. Ray was still nowhere to be found. Morgan noticed Bitty wanted out of Beth's arms. Apparently, Jake was more intriguing.

"Girl, are you okay?" Beth asked the poodle, checking out her legs, holding her like a baby, but Bitty was craning her neck toward Jake, squirming to get down.

"Okay, if that's what you want," Beth said. She clipped Bitty on her leash and let her down on the grass. "But be careful."

Jake sniffed Bitty from behind while Bitty allowed it, wagging her powderpuff tail, which encouraged Jake to lick the chocolate brown toy poodle, giving her a slimy bath.

"It looks like she might be okay," said Morgan, relieved. "But we could still go get the vet to check her out."

"I think she's just fine," Rick said, clasping a leash on Jake and bending down to pet him. Jake wagged his stubby tail. "So where do we sign? We really need to get back on the road. Need to find a place to spend the night maybe."

Morgan ushered the family and their dogs into the house and grabbed the adoption papers and a pen before they changed their mind. The Claytons met Ray, who never made outside and was chided by Morgan, Morgan thinking Ray could have somehow stopped the poodle from making her way to Daisy if he had only come outside.

"Now if for any reason you can't keep Jake, he will return to us at McAfee Mutts," Morgan said, circling the clause in the adoption papers, just to make sure they saw it. "We also like to make surprise visits at anytime, and this is where you okay us to do that."

"That seems a bit excessive," said Beth, looking as prissy as Bitty, who was sitting with her front legs crossed in her mistress's high-cotton content lap.

"It's only for the animal's protection," explained Morgan, trying to make eye contact with each family member. "We need to make sure they're safe and happy in your environment. I made many mistakes by not doing this with the animals I adopted to people. Also, please call us in a few days just to tell us how Jake is doing. And just keep us informed on how he's doing. We like to keep the lines of communication open."

Morgan looked at Jake, who was once again asleep and snoring. Only this time he was on a warm carpet. "His leg sometimes gives him a little more trouble in the wintertime," Morgan said, already missing Jake. "Nothing major, but he does love a massage in that leg sometimes. The vet told us that about him."

The new forever family got up to leave as Morgan bent down to kiss Jake one last time on his flat nose. She turned to shake Rick's hand, but saw Beth's disapproving look and smiled instead. Morgan's right cheek edged up far past her left one and Morgan didn't care. Morgan was happy for the first time since Lily had run away. "Welcome to the McAfee Mutt family," Morgan said.

Beatrice- Chapter 15

Beatrice, all puffed up like a proud mama, admired her shiny new animal board members that were sitting in the Fortville Police Department's community room, while Dotty, crocheting a star-spangled scarf for Pesto, sat beside her.

Beatrice would make damn sure there would be no talk of fixing anything except already established animal ordinances, the ones where you didn't have to fix your dog or pay to breed them. The Fortville City Council had voted to accept her recommendation that spaying and neutering should be *encouraged, not mandated* in Fortville. The second City Council vote on the damned ordinance was still months away. Tonight the animal board would discuss the Fortville Humane Society's contract with the city, which was set to expire in a month.

Beatrice looked around the room to see if Donna Martelli, the Fortville Humane Society director, had made it for what Beatrice feared might become a lynching with Derril Harmon at the helm. Harmon had practically voted himself in as chairman two weeks ago at the first meeting.

The dark-haired, slight Martelli sat in the back of the room along with a few of her staff, all dressed in pink t-shirts, like a flock of flamingos amidst a sea of red bloody wolves, the redshirts with audacity to show themselves at these meetings. Beatrice saw the local newspaper reporter, a handsome cub fresh off the journalism farm who couldn't spell his name correctly, and waved at him with her big hand. They had become good friends. He quoted her for newspaper articles from time to time.

Morgan McAfee was with her husband, who was talking as usual and wearing his stupid wire-frame glasses that kept falling down his nose. Beatrice tried not to stare at Morgan, who reminded her of a very attractive Australian shepherd. Beatrice finally tore herself away and plunged into her laptop, slamming her large hand on the mousepad to wake it up.

Dr. Peller, a veterinarian with beady little eyes that shifted behind thick Coke-bottle glasses circa 1967, was one of the animal board members who had worked on the animal committee with Beatrice. With a huge ego far surpassing his looks, he was said to be the cheapest vet in town, but Dr. Peller, of course, referred to himself as the thriftiest. Big Berta had taken her dogs to him for thirty years.

Dr. Shay, Beatrice's vet, was another animal board member who had also worked with Beatrice on the committee. He was a blond, blue-eyed vet who was what most would call handsome and had done more for the animal community than anyone in Fortville. He hardly ventured his opinion, being perceptive enough to know that folks around here had little tolerance for such trivialities.

A diversified set of people comprised the rest of the board, which ranged from animal advocates to an accountant to a lesbian, whom Beatrice thought was flirting with her thus prompting Beatrice to cut down on her lip balm for future meetings.

The police captain, a tall man with a burr haircut who reminded Beatrice of Sluggo from the comic strip *Nancy and Sluggo*, was in attendance in case the board had questions regarding city animal control.

And, of course there was Derril Harmon, with his red t-shirt and red reading glasses, thinking he looked so smart. Well, he just looked *red*.

"So, these are your euthanasia records?" Harmon asked, projecting upon a screen a euthanasia log depicting a list of the animals the Fortville Humane Society had euthanized for a particular month. "These reasons for euthanasia seem a bit ambiguous to me," Harmon said, like he was the king of the animal advocates. "If I were the one euthanizing these animals, I would detail the reasons a little better."

Martelli, sitting next to Harmon, looked as if she might cry. She was a puny little thing after all.

"Who makes the decision to euthanize these animals?" continued Harmon like he was Perry Mason.

"Several people like the shelter manager and myself, the director, maybe even the person who investigates cruelty if necessary and a vet, of course," Martelli said in a quiet voice, barely discernible. "It's an important group decision. Other people at the shelter are sometimes involved, too."

Harmon grabbed his readers off his head and twirled them around in his fingers. "Do you consult together? Everyone seeing the animal at the same time?"

Martelli laughed nervously. "Well, that would be hard to do with all our different schedules."

Harmon wouldn't give up. "So what would help you document these decisions better and how can we get the euthanasia rate down?"

Martelli looked down, for a moment, then lifted her pretty dark eyes, glaring at Harmon. "Money," Martelli said. "The animals deserve more medical attention, so more could stay alive. It just takes more money."

Harmon rolled his big bushy eyebrows up over his big bulgy eyes. "So how much more would it take?

Your budget is already almost three-hundred thousand dollars."

"Probably about another hundred thousand to help lower the rate of euthanasia."

The crowd sighed, their pockets already feeling the pinch.

"And what are the illnesses that would need to be treated with this money?" Harmon continued, spinning the damn glasses in his fingers again.

Martelli looked up, thinking. "Heartworms and distemper and parvovirus are the major canine killers. And the cats, I'd say feline leukemia is the reason why we have to put down a lot of those. We need more equipment and a vet full-time. Right now, we've only got a vet once a week."

Harmon, pushing his glasses back on his dyed head, looked at his notes then back at Martelli. "Donna, this not a witch hunt. What I want to do is to try to hammer out a good contract for both you and Fortville. There are too many animals and not enough homes. This, indeed, is the reason for your high numbers of euthanasia. It has nothing to do with lack of money," Harmon said as if he'd discovered the solution to world peace. "But we can only work with the instructions the city gives us to work with. And we want to give them new details to validate a lot of things we're trying to settle. We're not picking on you. We're just trying to understand." Harmon smiled at Martelli and patted her on the shoulder patronizingly. "But more money won't solve the problem."

"We need to address the cause," Dr. Peller interjected as he was want to do, always thinking he had something important to say. "We're dealing with the symptom."

"But you can't mandate spaying and neutering," offered up another board member, a very smart one apparently.

Martelli looked sick. "Truthfully, I think the reason that there is so much euthanasia is that these pet owners are not responsible for them. But they need to be educated too. Plus we need more legislation at citywide and statewide level. You've just got to make people more responsible."

Beatrice wondered what Martelli meant by that last remark. You couldn't fix irresponsible people. Hadn't Martelli read her blog? Beatrice needed to talk to Martelli and convince her to get rid of this Harmon. It shouldn't be too difficult after the way Harmon had treated her tonight, beating Martelli like a bad step dog.

Harmon looked proud of himself. "Well, I think and this animal board will agree that we've got to have more more definitive reasons for euthanasia and they should be more transparent. I think that the public should know. They have a right to know. They're paying for this."

"Donna Martelli doesn't make the decisions on the contract. She's not in charge of it, its board of directors are," said a voice from the audience. It was Dick Patterson, a board member of the Fortville Humane Society who served with Dotty.

Harmon pushed his readers back on his head and squinted in the direction of Patterson silhouetted against the fluorescent light. "What things would you like to see changed or amended on the contract, sir?" Harmon asked Patterson.

Patterson was quiet for a moment then stood up and sat back down. "I'm not sure. We're all new on the board," said Patterson.

"Poor Dick," said Dotty, taking a moment to look up from her crocheting then back down again. "It might help if he knew what he was talking about."

The board adjourned their meeting, with Harmon suggesting everyone visit the local animal shelter because they were doing the best they could despite all the dogs and cats that ended up there with most of them dying.

In the parking lot, Beatrice saw Harmon getting into his car.

"Derril Harmon drives a red Range Rover," said Beatrice, climbing into the car along with Dotty. "Who'd have thought?"

"Yes, who'd have thought that?" Dotty said, laughing. "I would have figured him for more of a red wagon man."

Beatrice looked into the rearview and started backing out.

"Beatrice, make sure you watch out for that pole there," said Dotty, craning her neck around and pointing back. "By the way, did you see that councilman L'Arion Middler was there tonight sitting in the back of the room?"

"No," said Beatrice, trying to ignore Dotty's contortions and concentrate. "Wonder why he was there?"

Dotty shook her frizzy-blonde head. "I guess he just wants to keep up with what's going on."

"How did he look?"

"He seemed a little upset to me."

"Really. Wonder why? Maybe he didn't like what went down tonight with Derril Harmon grilling Donna Martelli for dinner." Beatrice smiled big in her shiny teeth. "Guess he doesn't like Italian."

Winter

Lily-Chapter 16

Lily felt as if she would burst, her skin so tight. Sam, her boyfriend, was circling the frightened little Chinese-Crested, wondering what was wrong. She must have swallowed Tom, The Yellow-Striped Skinny Dog, the wretched thing hanging, by his claws, upside down inside of her.

She kneaded the blanket with her little paws and lay down, got back up, then lay down again, Lily not sure why. Suddenly, Lily felt a sharp pain in her backside and looked around to see a small dog, even smaller than Mortimer, falling out of her. Lily tried to stand back up to get a better look but couldn't, a heaviness seizing the little dog. Lily craned up her neck. It was The Shiny-Eyed holding her down.

Poor Lily lay helplessly until her curiosity got the best of her. She meekly raised her leg and looked. The tiny blob was wriggling around, groping blindly with its sharp claws. Lily licked it and tried to chew through its leash until The Shiny-Eyed, with her skinny paw, pinched its nose and tried to kill it.

Lily thought about biting The Shiny-Eyed until the pain crashed over her again. The little dog moaned and pushed until something again plopped itself upon the blanket. She licked it until it began to move.

Exhausted, Lily fell asleep to the rhythm of little paws kneading her belly. Surely, these new friends wouldn't mind if she nipped their backside. After all, they had come out of it.

Morgan-Chapter 17

Even the long-haired dogs shivered like the dickens in their kennels while Derril and Morgan, dressed in coveralls and heavy coats, staple-gunned sheets of plastic to the window facings of the shelter.

The only heat source in the shelter was a window unit in the laundry room that blew luke-warm air for a few minutes until it turned completely cold again. Volunteers used it to warm themselves in between tending to the dogs, although the volunteers didn't usually need to, so many dogs keeping the volunteers moving, the volunteers generating their own heat source.

Volunteers had little room to maneuver because the large kennels left only about of foot of space between them and the walls. Morgan and Derril stapled the plastic sheet to the window that had framed a muddy field of brown, a thicket of oak skeletons in the background, an unfinished chain-link fence in the foreground, a sky of slate risen to the top, frozen. They were both squeezed in tight to the window, straining to move.

"But what do you think they are going to ask me about?" Derril yelled above the barking dog din as he held up the sheet of plastic on the window. His back was flattened against the kennel containing the collie mix that had been abandoned at the dental office. The dog was fully restored and even feisty, jumping up and down.

Morgan leaned over sideways against Derril for support and staple-gunned the sheet of plastic around the window facing.

"Earth calling Morgan," Derril whispered loudly in Morgan's ear. "Why do you think the Fortville City Council wants a report so soon?"

The Fortville City Council, specifically Gary Rhodes, the vice mayor, had asked for a review of the new animal board's findings two months early, giving Derril less then two weeks to prepare one. The animal board had only been meeting for eight weeks.

"I'm worried," said Derril, yanking back his hand, Morgan almost stapling it. "What are you trying to do? Nail me to the wall like they are?" Derril grinned, his eyebrows popping up, his smudged, receding hairline disappearing under his stocking cap.

Morgan laughed and stepped back, smoothing the plastic with her hand. "I think it's just because, well..." Morgan began, shaking her head, silver wisps of hair falling over her ears, Morgan trying to grow out her hair. "I'm not sure, Derril, to be quite honest with you."

"Do you think I grilled the Fortville Humane Society director too much? That Donna Martelli. You were there. I just wanted to know the reasons why the animals were euthanized. Their reasons were very vague. They should at least use Asilomar Accords. Decent humane societies adhere to those. Especially ones that get paid by the city. Or they should."

Asilomar Accords was an established international classification system of data designed to create uniformity and understanding between animal welfare organizations. It included codification for euthanasias.

"She's stretching the truth anyway," Derril said, dragging, a few feet over, the plastic sheet that would go on the next window.

"What about?" Morgan asked, putting the staple gun into her pocket.

Derril shook his head. "She's fudging the euthanasia statistics. They're higher than she claims."

Donna Martelli had been reporting a lower euthanasia statistic than Billy Bob Sterling had quoted the City Council. Even the local paper reported Donna's differing numbers but never outright disputed her figures. To get to lower euthanasia numbers, Donna admitted to higher animal intake numbers, which was a real shame, no matter how one looked at it. And the new animal board, of which Derril was president, was having a hard time. One of its members had received a note on her car windshield that said, "I Put You Down," both grammar and message atrocious. Web discussion posts had also attacked Derril's character, questioning his integrity and background along with his qualifications to make animal welfare decisions on the animal board. Simply put, things weren't going too well.

   Derril stooped over and picked up a toy that the collie mix and Welsh Corgi had hurled out from under their kennel. "And this is weird, probably not a big deal," Derril said, tossing the toy back in. "But this white Prius keeps following me. I am getting paranoid, I think."

   Morgan maneuvered herself around the kennel, leaning under the book-reading lights that once were over nursing home beds, and wormed her way around the kennel and into the hallway. She motioned for Derril to follow her. "I think, well, you're doing great," Morgan said, trying to be positive. "After all, it was one of the animal committee's recommendations to require more transparency between the city and the humane society. You're doing that."

   Derril stuck his hand into the kennel to pet the border collie. "Plus, I apologized to Martelli for my tone, not for the questions I asked her, but for my tone," he said as the Welsh Corgi horned in, forcing Derril to give him some pets. Derril had taken the high road in the last animal board meeting and apologized to Donna, who had publicly accepted his apology, her peace offering making its way into the newspaper.

"Come on," Morgan said. "Let's go into the laundry room where we can talk better."

Morgan and Derril walked into the laundry room and closed the doors. Morgan turned on the window unit to get warm, wrapped her arms around herself and patted her body up and down to generate some body heat while Derril took the bedding and towels out of the dryer.

"Derril, just throw them in the bin," Morgan said, blowing her breath on her hands to warm them.

"They need to be folded," Derril said. "Mouse said so." He wiped off the dog hair first, dropped the clean towels on top of the dryer, then started folding.

Morgan cleared her throat. "Derril, I don't think you *grilled* her, like people, some of the Fortville Council people, are saying. You were just getting to the truth."

Derril dropped the towels on the dryer as if he'd been shocked by an electric current, Morgan worrying for a split-second that Ray had mis-wired the dryer. "The truth is that I had a bad experience at that Fortville shelter," Derril said, his voice low, Morgan still straining to hear him. "They euthanized a dog that I had wanted to foster, saying it was sick, but I know it wasn't."

Morgan walked over to Derril and patted him on his shoulder. She had gone through a similar experience there, though she had managed to rescue her Charlie.

Specifically, Derril had told Donna that he was sorry for the tone of voice he had used to question her, but he had qualified that same apology by saying he wasn't sorry for asking the hard questions. Morgan and Ray thought that an apology, even a qualified one, was an admission of guilt. The McAfees thought like their dogs: An exposed soft belly, helpless and juicy, signified weakness, making it ripe for the taking.

A piercing yelp catapulted Morgan and Derril out of the laundry room. The doberman, Dobie, was attacking a German shepherd in the kennel they had shared for three months. He had pinned the shepherd down on its back to the cement floor and was mauling the poor thing, a gaping hole in his neck.

Morgan grabbed a heavy leash and ran into the kennel. She tried but failed to get it around the doberman's neck as he slung the poor shepherd's body from side to side, the yellowed floral wallpaper splattered with thick crimson.

Beatrice-Chapter 18

Beatrice swiveled into her best pair of black jeans and pulled on her finest black turtleneck. She even fancied up her short red hair a little, gelling it extra high toward heaven because one might actually exist.

Derril Harmon was getting hanged today.

Vice Mayor Gary Rhodes had requested that Harmon give a progress report, bumping up the report prematurely by two months, today at the Fortville City Council's noon study session at the library. But Beatrice knew that was a only a ruse and instead the fur was going to hit the fan for Harmon's behavior at the last animal board meeting when he had raked Donna Martelli over the coals. This might be the last of Derril Harmon, the bug-eyed nuisance. Beatrice certainly hoped so.

She zipped up her black sweatshirt and petted Bay-Bay and Rihanna, both in matching Dobermans Suck hoodies. She tucked her lunch into her satchel and walked out the door, ducking her head under the low door casing of the post-modern house. She folded her long tall self into her Prius and started her drive into work, pulling on to the bricked streets of the quaint neighborhood.

Swerving to miss all the gray-hairs out for their morning walks, Beatrice smiled when she saw the note from Dotty taped to her console that said "I love you." Dotty, who didn't have a car, had borrowed the Prius car last night for one of her late-night craft binges.

Beatrice looked up and saw Ben in his driveway, which was only a couple of blocks from Beatrice's house. He was climbing into his old Chevy Luv, the truck tricked out with new racing tires, the one and only perk of tire store management.

Beatrice pulled her car behind Ben's truck and parked. She left the engine on to keep it warm, opened her door, got out and walked up to Ben's truck. She hadn't seen Ben in several months, not since the dog show, which was unusual. Beatrice and Ben usually got together at least once a week.

Ben's yellow tomcat was on top of the roof looking down, surveying his domain. Beatrice hated cats and never could understand her brother's love for them.

"What's going on, brother?" Beatrice asked, tapping on Ben's truck window, scaring Ben to death, Ben apparently not hearing her drive up.

Ben, visibly shaken, rolled down his window. "Not much, how about you?" asked Ben, trying to smile.

Beatrice looked in the car garage window. "Where's Reba's car? She already gone to work?"

"Yeah, I guess so," Ben replied calmly before self-combusting into tears, his little pick-up convulsing with big Ben's every sob. "Oh, Bea, Reba left me. She took everything. Even the dog."

Beatrice put her big hand on Ben's big shoulder. "Oh, lord, Ben, you sound like a bad country song. I thought she didn't even like those dogs."

"*Dog.* I only had the boy. The girl was gone a long time ago. I think Reba took her and did something with her, too. She did it to spite me."

Ben blew his nose on his pocket handkerchief so hard that the truck began convulsing again.

Beatrice punched a hole out of the cold air with her large fist. "Only Reba could be mean enough to do that. Go down to the police station and charge Reba with stealing. Talk to Kendra. She's a cop. I know her. She'll help you."

Ben, cowering, afraid his sister might punch him, too, looked up at Beatrice. "But I think the dogs are in both of our names. I think they're in hers too. But I'll check the registration."

Beatrice waved him off like she was heading up a wagon train then suddenly froze in place, putting her fist up to her chin. "No, first get their AKC certificates and go down there to the police station for proof. Get it together. And stop your blubbering. Do something about this."

"Okay. I will."

Beatrice, thankful for her thermal socks on such a frigid day, jogged back to her car, her Birkenstocks flip-flopping along the way. She got in the car and continued her drive into work. It was going to be good day today if she had to force it.

The grand library, with its topless rotunda, had always annoyed Beatrice. To her, it seemed unfinished, like the builders, on the verge of completing the beautiful temple to the Book God, ran out of money. Or, perhaps, barbaric invaders from the north just killed them. Beatrice surmised that the incomplete rotunda was the reason why the library was always asking for more money from the taxpayers, never finishing it no matter how much money they got.

Early for the study session, Beatrice walked through the doors at the ground level of the unfinished rotunda and into the cafe, where she ordered a cinnamon latte with an extra shot of expresso. She had already prepared her lead for her blog about today's study session but wanted to work on it a little more.

Suddenly, Derril Harmon walked in, and Beatrice, ordering a cookie from the girl at the counter, lost her appetite, a first for Beatrice.

"Would you like anything else?" asked the counter girl, concerned, Beatrice's white face turning even whiter.

"No, I'm good," Beatrice said, a bit discombobulated and pivoting straight into Harmon standing right behind her, Beatrice unaware of his close proximity. Giving

Harmon an extra-long glare, Beatrice side-stepped him like a piece of chewed-up tobacco on the sidewalk. She walked slowly to a table and cooly looked around, expecting Harmon to be staring at her. He wasn't, Beatrice deducing it to be some sort of tactical maneuver. As Harmon sat down at a table a few feet away, Beatrice pulled her lunch sack from her satchel and in a split second, Beatrice not even realizing how she got there, was opposite him. Harmon looked at her like he didn't know who she was, but Beatrice was sure he knew who she was.

Harmon was stuffing his face with a biscotti, his huge jaws like a mechanical cow eating a cud. "Can I help you?"

"Yeah, I think you can," Beatrice said, taking a deep breath. "I just want to ask if you have an agenda. It seems like you do."

Harmon acted innocent. "What do you mean, *agenda*?"

Beatrice cocked her invisible guns under the table, hoping Harmon would hear them. "*We* specifically said, I mean the *animal committee said,* that mandating spay/neuter would not help lower the amount of homeless animals. Why do you keep pursuing it? The city says you have eleven recommendations to work on. Well, making somebody neuter or spay their dog isn't one of them."

"I am trying to make the local humane society more transparent, so we can work with them," Harmon replied. "*That is* one of your recommendations. Don't you remember writing it?"

Beatrice pulled the triggers on both her guns. "You have an agenda to push--the spay/neuter ordinance. To convince people that's what needs to happen. Don't you?"

Harmon looked panicked. "The only agenda I have is to help the animals. This is just a suggestion, but why don't you do the same? I understand you're an animal lover."

"*You're* the one who needs to tell the truth. Not Donna Bartelli who *is* telling the truth. You're not helping a bit," Beatrice said, getting up and walking to her table. She stuffed her lunch back into her satchel along with her invisible guns, still smoking. There was nothing more to say.

Lily-Chapter 19

When Lily's two new friends had wiggled out of her backside, Sam, Lily's boyfriend, was still in the crying cage where The Shiny-Eyed had tossed him. He was with that silly Sally, who wasn't nearly as pretty as Lily. Sam was constantly barking, proclaiming his love for Lily and only Lily, though she had once caught Sam sniffing Sally's backside.

But Lily was really much too busy to worry about Sam. She had two new friends, after all. Little Mort was quite a clown. He looked like a tiny Lily in pink skin and white fur and black spots. Lily watched as he dumped over the water bowl, a solid chunk of ice falling out.

Samson, a miniature version of Sam, with long silver-gray hair, sat on his haunches with his lovely ears perked high, snowflakes melting on his perfect warm nose. Samson was the thinker of the bunch.

Lily nipped Little Mort on his backside and turned and ran in the other direction as fast as her little feet could take her, but Little Mort caught her quickly, Lily not as fast as she used to be. Little Mort baited Samson to join in the game by nudging the pup and in response, Samson squeaked his delight, which concerned Lily, Lily none too fond of squeaks.

So, Lily demonstrated, in her biggest voice, how to bark correctly. The pups, rapt, suddenly stopped their play, turning both of their beautiful faces toward her, their fine ears perked up, and listened. Lily, who had never taught anyone anything before, enjoyed telling her new friends what to do. She might learn to like it here with The Shiny-Eyed.

Morgan-Chapter 20

Morgan, with Ray right behind her, arrived at the library in a bit of a bluster. It was just a few minutes before the special session where Derril would give his report. Morgan had tried to get there earlier to encourage Derril, but Nelda had detained Morgan at the dental office, complaining about Morgan's leaving early, which, ironically, had kept Morgan at the office even longer. Morgan also had to stop by the shelter to talk to the dogcatcher about his picking up puppies without their mothers. Morgan insisted the mothers be picked up in addition to the puppies, with the hopes of stopping more irresponsible breeding, dog owners tossing their mixed-breed puppies to shelters while keeping their purebred puppies to sell.

In the lobby leading to the community room, a local television crew was taping a few of the McAfee Mutt volunteers before the special session started. One of the volunteers had sent out a press release and followed up with personal calls. The effort had netted one measly media bite.

"Ms. McAfee, you're just in time," the pretty reporter said, ushering Morgan between the two other volunteers as the cameraman did a sound check with them.

Morgan hated being in front of the camera but had learned to accept it as her obligation to try to help the homeless animals. She had learned though to be careful with what she said to them. The media wanted a happy, uncomplicated story or a very sad, dramatic one, both of them usually unrealistic. People just brought more dogs to McAfee Mutts after seeing Morgan in the news.

"One unaltered female can produce sixty-seven thousand dogs in seven years," Morgan said, keeping her focus on the reporter, trying not to think about her scars, which always made her self-conscious. "The fingers need to be pointed to the City of Fortville. They are the only ones who can make difference in numbers of animals euthanized every year by implementing spay/neuter laws. Education is important, too. It should start early in the schools."

After the interview, as the cameraman unplugged Morgan's and the volunteers' wireless mics, the reporter said the story would air that night. Morgan was hopeful and needed for their side of the story to be told; the media, so far, had not told any of it.

Morgan looked around the community room of the library and saw a few red-shirts but not nearly enough for what she thought was going to happen.

The community library room was big and nice and new and filled to the rim with people. Morgan didn't know anyone except for the volunteers and Donna, the Fortville Humane Society director. Donna was whispering into Gary Rhodes' ear, which was so big it could probably discern the fluorescent lights' buzzing two stories up. Morgan wondered what she could be telling him. She also saw Billy Bob, with whom she had become friends. Morgan had taken several dogs and cats from him that needed homes, his spay/neuter clinic quickly becoming an animal shelter.

Mayor Col. Sanders was tapping his microphone, signaling for the meeting to begin. All the city leaders were sitting around three long tables shaped in a U in front of the room. Lance Blackmon and Anne Meyers were smiling and talking with one another, which Morgan took as a good sign. At least Lance's eye wasn't blinking.

Derril had polished his ten pages of the animal board's progress until they shined and sent copies to all the city leaders, including the mayor and city administrator. Derril wanted everyone to be prepared.

"Shall we pray?" asked councilman Fleming, kicking off the meeting. Morgan remembered that Fleming was the only city leader who didn't think people should be held responsible for their dog pooping in some else's yard, actually voting against this recommendation from the animal committee. Morgan considered taking one of her dogs over to his yard to poop in it, wondering what his response would be then, betting it wouldn't be a prayer.

The council recited the pledge of allegiance, and the mayor read the agenda items. Gary Rhodes, red-faced, looking as if his big ears might blow out steam, called Derril for the report. Morgan wished she could have gotten to the study session earlier to encourage Derril, whose hands shook as he sat down. Morgan silently said a prayer for him.

Derril wore a nicely starched red shirt and blue jeans, obviously pressed by his mother, who was beaming in the audience like Derril was the new Jesus. He cleared his throat and smiled at the Council, who were all staring at their computer notepads with the exception of Anne Meyers, Lance and Buddy Bateman, who, at least, smiled back.

Derril looked at his notes and cleared his throat again. Morgan wished she could speak for him. "The city's animal board has been meeting for eight weeks and here's a summary of what we've done so far on the animal committee's eleven recommendations to the City Council." Derril cleared his throat again, his voice cracking, and continued. "One of the recommendations was greater transparency of the local humane society's reporting of reasons for euthanasia, which we have found are vague, and euthanasia statistics, which we have found are unclear..."

Donna was smiling. Sitting beside her was Dick Patterson, her board president. Patterson had made a public display at the last animal board meeting by standing and claiming that Donna didn't have the authority to speak on the Fortville Humane Society's contract with the city, and the only ones qualified were Humane Society board members themselves. Ironically, Patterson had also said he hadn't been on the Board long enough to know the answers when Derril had questioned him. Morgan thought that the outburst was totally out of line and unsolicited because Derril, at the start of the meeting, had asked audience members to remain quiet during the animal board meeting, a request that Patterson had blatantly denied.

"...and another recommendation was restructuring the contractual support of the local humane society," Derril continued, his voice getting clearer and stronger, as if gathering confidence with the words he spoke.

"The animal board has found that the local humane society's financial support from Fortville is growing, and we believe that they should become more dependent on their fundraisers and grants as recommended by the United States Humane Society. But it is not their fault. It is because of the overwhelming number of animals coming into their shel--"

"What has happened is that you and your animal board have overstepped your boundaries," Gary Rhodes interrupted, the steam obvious, Morgan feeling its thickness on her skin. "There are eleven items that the animal committee recommended. And intense interrogation of the Fortville Humane Society for two hours in a public forum doesn't even begin to correlate with those eleven items."

Derril looked up from his notes as if he'd been smacked by a two-by-four.

"There are *two* items," Rhodes continued, holding up two of his long, bony fingers, his face getting redder and redder. "*Two* of the *eleven* that have to do with reporting and transparency of the Fortville Humane Society. You should have worked more cooperatively with them for the information that was needed."

Morgan steeled herself in her chair. Ray, sensing her anger, reached over with his arm, pressing it against Morgan. Morgan turned her head and glared at Ray and looked back at Derril. Ray retracted his arm slowly from across her chest.

"I did publicly make amends to Ms. Martelli," Derril said, trying to explain. "I sincerely said I was sorry for the way I delivered my questions. It isn't uncommon to have a bad thing happen to someone at the local humane society. Well, that happened to me. Unfortunately, my tone wasn't the best that night. But I wasn't out to prove that they weren't doing the job."

L'Arion Middler, in his dreadlocks with a Choctaw Nation bandanna wrapped around them, weighed in. "I could hardly bear what was happening at that meeting. It was like you didn't even give Ms. Martelli a chance to explain what happens there."

Morgan thought L'Arion should spend some time at McAfee Mutts instead of at city meetings. His delicate constitution was apparently not strong enough to withstand politics.

"But the second meeting went better," Derril countered. "We're moving forward. We want to work with them. We're on their side."

Rhodes tried hard to compose himself, but the gasket had already blown, the steam all over him and everybody else. "We've given you some wiggle room to look at the laws for animals in this city, and I appreciate that effort, but that shouldn't give you permission to interrogate the head of the local humane society. I take issue at that point. It's not the city's job to run the Fortville Humane Society. You need to be an advisory board and not redo everything the animal committee has already done."

"Would you like the animal board to just be a rubber stamp, without any further research, facts or opinions?" Derril asked as Morgan's mouth flopped open.

Rhodes jammed his glasses up on his nose, possibly generating more steam to blow out of his ears, and glared at Derril. "I would like for you to wrap up its report in *four weeks*," Rhodes finally said, his lips so tight the words barely got out.

"Then why did you, Mr. Rhodes, commission some of its members with terms of *one to three* years?" Derril shot back. "And it was you, sir, who voted for it to be an ongoing board to act in an advisory capacity to the Mayor and City Council."

"Derril, you were charged with getting the facts and to make recommendations back to the board," Lance said, trying to come to Derril's rescue, his left eye starting to twitch. "You can't do that without the facts. I applaud you for getting in there and digging for the facts."

L'Arion Middler spoke again, his muscular arms planted across his chest defensively. "The pet owner should be responsible for fixing his pet. Not us, this City Council, in regard to spaying and neutering."

The room was silent as if a bomb had just detonated and this was the calm before the chaos. Morgan looked around for victims but saw none. Most were acting as if nothing had happened, Morgan wondering why. She hadn't seen too many dogs that had been treated worse than Derril had been today in this room by so-called city leaders.

"And now for the second item on the agenda," Mayor Bell droned while Derril got up and headed for the door.

Morgan jumped up with Ray right behind her, Ray afraid of what she might do.

"Derril, wait," Morgan said, running into the lobby.

Derril stopped and turned, looking panicked.

Morgan walked up and hugged him, feeling him tremble. "Derril, you did great," Morgan said, leaning back to look at Derril, her hands still on his shoulders. "You told them the facts. I'm so proud of you."

"Morgan, I was scared to death," Derril said, his face as red as his shirt. "You think I did all right? I tried to hold my own."

"Why do you insist on telling lies instead of the truth, Mr. Harmon?" Morgan heard a voice say. It was Dick Patterson, his chiseled features harsh in the cool blue light of winter flooding through the window of the hallway.

"You leave him alone," Morgan said, putting her arm around Derril and leading him outside. Derril didn't need to respond to that kind of behavior.

Morgan said her good-byes to Derril and that she would email him later to check on him. She looked forward to the news interview that they had done. That would make it better. Derril had done such a good job defending himself. People would see the truth. She had a lot of other messes to clean up, mainly ones created by dogs. Morgan did not have time for human messes.

Beatrice-Chapter 21

"You should have been there at that special study session yesterday. The one that Gary requested," Beatrice said to Dotty. The two were having having dinner at Beatrice's. Bay-Bay, Rihanna and Pesto were crunching on their own bowl of fancy doggy treats under the dining room table. "And at the animal board meeting tonight, it looked like Derril Harmon was crashing. He even asked me if I had anything to add.

Well, I was out in the audience just like I always am taking notes on my laptop." Beatrice, unusually tipsy, laughed and slapped her leg with her big hand. "I told him 'not at this time' very cooly cause you know how cool I am. I don't think he'll be on the animal board much longer. If he doesn't get taken down first, he'll just have to resign."

Derril Harmon's upbraiding by Councilman and Vice-Mayor Gary Rhodes was all over the front page of the Fortville newspaper and the Web. It looked like Harmon had cooked his own goose if Gary hadn't cooked it for him. The damned spay/neuter vote had been tabled for a second time like the vampire that would never die, the crucifix not plunged straight into its heart despite the hero's wholehearted efforts. It was scheduled for a second Council vote in a few weeks, but the ordinance was going down with a capital D since Harmon got into all this mess. Beatrice couldn't have planned it any better.

Dotty, in a red-white-and-blue sweater she had just crocheted the night before, poured herself a second glass of wine. "Don't you think you're taking this a little too seriously, Bea?" Dotty asked, swirling her wine in her glass. "Or maybe you're not taking it seriously enough? I mean, these animal shelter people get a lot of grief, just like me. I work with homeless people. They work with homeless animals. It's called compassion fatigue, Bea. It's textbook."

Beatrice jumped up from the table waving her big hands. "What's that supposed to mean? *You're* the one that got me involved in this. Why did we waste all that time on the animal committee with those recommendations if the City Council wasn't going to listen to them?"

Dotty screwed up her face as if she might cry.

Beatrice's barking email alert on her cell phone punctuated the awkward silence. She looked at her phone and grabbed it. "Oh, my gosh, what have we here? Looks like I've got something from Harmon. Why on earth would he be emailing me?" Beatrice asked, tapping the phone's screen, fumbling with her big fingers for the correct email.

Beatrice opened it and read it silently while Dotty fed leftover steak to Pesto. "We'll just work out a little harder tomorrow, my little Italian stallion," Dotty said, petting Pesto, giving him bits of steak that she had chewed up first. Bay-Bay and Rihanna watched, saliva dripping from their open mouths. Beatrice didn't think

Dotty should feed Pesto table scraps, but Dotty did it anyway, sometimes just to spite Beatrice.

Since Pesto's big win, Dotty had been considering quitting her social welfare job as a Homeless Angel and becoming a professional dog handler on the national dog show circuit. Now when she wasn't crocheting, knitting or paper crafting, Dotty had begun training Pesto intensively by holding the little dog upright and bouncing him on a mini-trampoline although Dotty was careful not to feed him first. She had learned the hard way about Pesto's delicate digestive needs. The little dog had upchucked on too many of her sweaters.

"So, what does the email say?" Dotty said, getting up and gathering the dishes. "Tell me, I guess."

"Well, Derril Harmon is telling Gary and everyone else on the City Council, including me for some reason, how he so appreciated the public spanking he got yesterday at the study session and how he tried not to say *spay/neuter* at the animal board meeting tonight because it was a dirty word that Gary had told him not to say." Silently, Beatrice read a little further down. "And he tells Gary good luck with that run for mayor.

He's voting for him. All said facetiously, of course. Pretty darned funny actually and well-written."

Beatrice read the rest of the letter to herself, chuckling, while Dotty rinsed off the dishes in the sink.

"Okay, tell me more," Dotty said, her interest piqued despite her prickled conscience.

"Here Harmon says, how foolish he is, calling himself this little old boy raised on a farm, to think he knows anything about animals or statistics. He mentions his degree from a university and blah-blah-blah."

"Sounds like he's pretty hurt, actually," Dotty said, starting the dishwasher.

"*Pretty hurt*, bah. Sounds like he's *pretty crazy* to me." Beatrice put her phone in her black sweatshirt pocket and got up, heading for her bedroom. "I better go blog about this. This is priceless. You can't make up stuff this good."

Dotty jumped in front of Beatrice then plopped down on the sofa, patting the empty seat beside her. "Hey Beatrice, I thought we were going to watch some television. There's an *L Word* rerun tonight."

"Sorry. I gotta get this done," Beatrice said, not even trying to break her stride. But suddenly Beatrice felt guilty. "Raincheck, okay?"

Dotty grabbed up Pesto, scaring the little dog to death, and stomped out the door, her orthopedic shoes not making much noise despite Dotty's best efforts. She slammed the door behind her while Beatrice, reclining against the bedroom door facing, waited for Dotty's reappearance. The familiar frizzy-blonde head and Pesto's quivering little pointed nose weren't long in again presenting themselves. Dotty looked apologetic. "Bea, can I borrow your car? I gotta run an errand. Go to Craftmart."

"Sure, I don't need it," Beatrice said, grabbing the car keys off the coffee table and tossing them to Dotty. "I've got lots of writing to do."

"Thanks, I appreciate it," Dotty replied, catching the keys one-handed then closing the door with poor little Pesto's pointed nose.

The following morning, Beatrice, squeezed into her cubicle at Computerville, talked to Ben on her cellphone. "What do you mean?" Beatrice barked. "The police are telling you that they can't arrest Reba?

That's insane. She stole your dog. Hell, she stole two of your dogs."

"Bea," Ben replied, his voice calm, trying his best not to get Beatrice riled up. "I talked to Kendra at the police department, and she said I couldn't report Fredo as stolen because Fredo is in both our names."

Beatrice kicked the bottom of her cubicle with her sandaled foot causing her Birkenstock to go flying across the office. She grimaced. "Why did you tell the truth? Why didn't you say he was just in your name."

Ben was silent for a second. "Bea, I couldn't lie like that. I checked the American Dog Club registration. Both our names were on it."

The employee in the next cubicle got up and walked away, glaring at Beatrice as he did so. Beatrice glared back at him. "What's the matter with you?" Beatrice interrogated the employee. Beatrice yanked her attention back to Ben. "But who knows what kind of danger that dog is in?"

"Reba won't hurt him. She's just mad for some reason at me. It will blow over. Well, anyway, since Fredo was both Reba's and mine, its technically not stealing the dog."

"Well, that's the stupidest thing I ever heard. I'm going down there to talk to Kendra myself. You put it on Facebook that Reba's missing. And Fredo. And even Lily. Let's get people looking for all of them, the dogs and Reba."

"Well, that might scare Reba away. She's on Facebook all the time."

"Well, that might not be a bad thing, scaring her away. Do it, Ben."

"Okay. But what about the dogs? Or the dog. Or the dogs."

"I will find them somehow. What I want to know is why you waited so long? That makes it harder to find them."

Ben paused again. "I didn't want to alarm you. It's embarrassing. To have your wife leave you. And, for that matter your dogs."

"Your dogs didn't leave you. She took them away from you, that dog-stealing snakestress. I'll talk to you later. Now standby your phone. Give me Reba's license plate number."

"Okay," Ben said, rattling a paper. "It's Arkansas 578-###. Got that?"

"Got it." Beatrice shot out of her cubicle, jumped in her Prius and sped, sans seatbelt, to the police department. Beatrice, on a mission, had never exceeded the speed limit, let alone minus a seatbelt.

Kendra, behind the admissions desk, was checking a thug into custody, another cop helping her, when Beatrice stumbled in.

"Kendra, you've got to help me," Beatrice said, out of breath, falling out of her sandal and going back to retrieve it. "Ben told me what you told him."

"Bea, there's nothing I can do. Technically it's Ben's wife's dog too. She's not stealing."

Beatrice hugged Kendra, accidentally getting the thug in her bear grasp too. "Please, please," Beatrice begged. "I've got to find this dog for my brother. It's about all he's got left."

"Beatrice, there's nothing I can do," Kendra said, wrenching Beatrice off her. She clasped the handcuffs on the thug, bending his arms behind his back and twisting his wrists.

"Sure there is," Beatrice ventured. "How about finding her van? She's got a cell phone and a license plate. Can't we track her?"

Kendra handed the thug over to the other cop then pulled Beatrice outside the automated doors of the police station. Kendra was almost as big as Beatrice. "Look, there may be something I can do," Kendra said. She retrieved a crunched cigarette just mangled in the fray from her shirt pocket and lit it. "If you promise not to to make a fuss."

"Okay," Beatrice said, moving out of Kendra's smoke, Kendra either forgetting or ignoring Beatrice's cigarette aversion. "Scout's honor. I'm listening."

"Give me her license plate number and her cell-phone number."

"Okay," Beatrice said, pulling the information out of her pocket as if on cue and trying not to cough. "Thank you."

Kendra took a drag on her cigarette and blew her smoke into the winter cold. "I can't promise anything."

Beatrice shook her head and looked down. "And I'm sorry I treated you so badly, Kendra. I really am. About that night that we were together and I never called you back. It wasn't right. I should've called you."

"It's okay, it wasn't that big a deal, Beatrice, you didn't break my heart. I lived. I'm dating a really nice social worker now."

"Oh. That's good."

"But thank you for apologizing. It means a lot. Now get out of here," Kendra said, dropping her cigarette into the ashcan and walking into the police station.

Beatrice had just gotten into her car when she got a call on her cell phone. It was Kendra. "Beatrice, we found Reba. She's at the River Park."

"Thank you!" yelled Beatrice.

"You bet. Keep in touch."

Beatrice pushed down the accelerator and squealed out of the police department parking lot. A policeman shook his finger at her, but Beatrice ignored it.

Beatrice arrived at the park and looked around, not seeing much of anything except homeless people with homeless dogs sitting at a picnic table. Beatrice got some change out of her satchel and walked up to the man and boy sitting opposite one another at a picnic table, dogs eating peanut butter sandwiches underneath the table. Beatrice thought about Dotty, knowing it was she who had fed these people and their animals. Gratefulness washed over Beatrice, an unfamiliar feeling she misinterpreted for humidity.

"Hey, have you all seen a white van?" Beatrice asked the boy, who was surprisingly well-dressed, wearing a new Northern Exposure jacket.

"Yeah, right behind that tree thicket up there," answered the old man instead, his gnarled finger pointing toward the river at a bunch of pin oak trees. "She has us get her and her little dog food all the time."

Beatrice looked in the direction the old man was pointing and saw a white van pulling out of the thicket onto the highway. Beatrice had run all they way back to her car before forgetting she had money for the homeless. She returned full speed, tossing the coins in her wake, accidentally hitting the old man in the face with a quarter.

Then Beatrice, mouthing "I'm sorry," wheeled and ran toward her car. She jumped into it, opting again for no seatbelt again, and peeled onto the highway.

She drove until she saw the white van stopped at an intersection, the *I love Chinese-Cresteds* bumper sticker staring straight at her.

"What a lie that is," said Beatrice. She tailed the van loosely for several minutes until the van pulled into an alley, a black SUV parked in it. Beatrice drove past, keeping her distance and parked a few hundred yards away in front of an old abandoned drug store. She got out of the car and walked quietly, as quietly as Beatrice could, to the edge of the old building and peeked around the corner.

Reba, dressed in large jeans that looked borrowed and an extra large sweatshirt, hopped out of the van with little grey-and-white spotted Fredo, a powderpuff (Big Berta hated this word) Chinese-Crested in her arms. A well-dressed woman in dark sunglasses was walking toward them. Reba handed Fredo to the woman.

"Halt, I say, stop!" Beatrice yelled, charging into the alley and pulling her invisible guns out of her pocket, Reba beginning to run.

"Stop, Reba, I've got a gun," Beatrice said, kicking off her Birkenstock sandals and running sock-footed down the alleyway, but Reba was already peeling out with the van.

Reba was long gone before Beatrice sat atop the woman with dark sunglasses. Fredo almost got away before Beatrice tackled him, giving the woman an escape opportunity. The woman in the dark sunglasses scrambled up, high heels and all, hightailing it in her fancy diamond-backed jeans to her black SUV, a stream of high-pitched cursing ripping through the frigid air behind her.

Spring

Lily-Chapter-22

The sun was high above the crying cage. The many smells were lush and overwhelming. The Shiny-Eyed, blowing her smoke breath, babbling in her high-pitched noises, was looking at Lily. The little Chinese-Crested wondered what she wanted. The Shiny-Eyed didn't come around much.

Lily lay on on her back, played dead and sat up and counted, barking once for Samson and once for Little Mort. But The Shiny-Eyed still wouldn't go away.

So Lily, not knowing what else to do, padded to the bowl to get a drink of water. Suddenly, Little Mort knocked her down, the pup charging for the bowl, burrowing his nose under it spilling water everywhere. The Shiny-Eyed swooped into the crying cage and swatted Little Mort on his backside, and just as quickly as she came in, picked up the bowl and disappeared.

Lily, hoping the storm blown past, watched Little Mort lick The Shiny-Eyed's sting, Samson, his brother nuzzling him.

Then, a bowl of fresh water in her paw, The Shiny-Eyed came back. Little Mort headed for the bowl until The Shiny-Eyed grabbed him by the scruff of his neck and dangled the poor pup, squirming, in the air. Samson, his little ears laid back, watched helplessly.

Lily clamped her teeth upon The Shiny-Eyed and shook her tufted head with all her might until The Shiny-Eyed yelped and dropped Little Mort. Lily tried to reach the little pup before The Shiny-Eyed picked up Lily and tossed her against the cage, but Lily was too late.

Lily opened her eyes just in time to watch The Shiny-Eyed's long paws clutch Little Mort and Samson and take them away.

When The Big Noisy Thing growled, Lily knew her new friends would never be back. Lily cried until she fell asleep to Sam's moans under the big moon.

Morgan-Chapter 23

In between all her dog doings, Morgan watched the local news every night for a week to see the television interview they had taped, but it never aired. The volunteer initiating the interview had called the media and asked the reason why the story hadn't made the cut but hadn't received any solid answers other than the standard time factor excuse. But the answer was there, in the back of their minds, like an invisible boogie man one couldn't quite get a bead on. And the name of that boogie man was the City of Fortville.

Derril's resignation from the animal board made front page news. Morgan had insisted that Derril remain on the animal board, that he could do a lot of good for animals by staying, but Derril, claiming the damage had already been done, said he would work for the animals in other ways.

Gary Rhodes had made a statement, also front page news, in which he called Derril's e-mail a personal attack on him and that Derril, instead, should be working cooperatively toward achieving the goals of the Fortville City Council, even though the goals were never made clear.

To make Derril out to be an even worse villain, the vice president of the animal board had also been quoted in the same front page story, saying how ashamed she was of Derril's behavior, apologizing for it to city leaders. But Lance, Anne Meyers and Buddy Bateman, remained supportive, calling Derril's report thorough and informative with the animal board itself heading in the right direction.

It was one bad deal and Morgan felt for Derril, who now slept, not only with a sleeping mask but a baseball bat since someone had let out his six dogs during Derril's final animal board meeting. After several long hours, Derril had found all six of the frightened dogs running down the middle of the busiest road in Fortville, miles away from his house. They were all okay but could have been killed.

Also, Derril was still getting hammered via message boards, letters to the editor and Beatrice Cooper's damn blogs that criticized Derril as if he had pissed upon the city leaders and not cleaned up his mess, Councilman Fleming not included, of course. Derril had been portrayed as a crazy man, and Morgan wondered if he might not become a crazy man after so much public scrutiny.

Since it was newly spring, Morgan was taking the plastic off the shelter windows. The dogs, in their kennels, were lying on their bellies in their precious swatch of sunlight, when Morgan heard someone banging on the door. Morgan dropped her fencing pliers and made her way around the kennels into the hallway and pushed open the heavy door. It was the mean old man in the wheelchair, the one with the rotting leg from diabetes, the one who always complained about the noise.

    Morgan was not prepared for his complaints. She had a couple of adoptions today and needed to clean the shelter. Morgan tried to smile, faking it a bit. "Hi, what can I do for you? I'm sorry about the dogs," Morgan said, trying to look apologetic and waving her arms toward the kennels to each side of the hallway. "I think they're just excited I'm here. They'll quiet down when I leave."

    "Oh, that's okay," the old man said. Spittle of some sort ran down the sides of his cheeks and a liter of pop sat in his wheelchair caddy. "I came looking for my dog? He got out. Wife let him out. Do you think you might have him?" Morgan had just gotten several warnings from the Multown police department about the noise from the animal shelter. She was pretty sure that the old man was behind those warnings.

    The neighborhood cats had also been dropping like flies. Morgan assumed their nine lives were cut short by the old man poisoning them. A little old lady, who lived near the shelter, had recently died and left a lot of cats to fend for themselves, so Morgan had been trapping as many of them as she could before he killed them. She had transferred most of them, via the van, to her barn, now a big cat colony. The kids' old tractor tire outside was filled with kitty litter.

As she looked at the pitiful old man, Morgan tried to not think of the syringes of sodium pentobarbital in the refrigerator. She would need a lot of them to put down this old geezer, who wasn't worth the drugs and needles it would take to kill him anyway. "So what's your dog look like?" Morgan asked, pulling down her ball cap, motioning him in anyway. "Come on in."

"He's a chihuahua, little bitty thing. Mean," he said, starting up his wheelchair then motoring into the shelter as Morgan held open the door. He was in raggedy sweats that smelled worse than the dogs. Morgan pinched her nose as the door slammed behind her.

The old man stopped by every room, peering in hopefully, until he found what he was looking for. Laughing, his bare belly shaking under the dirty waistband of his sweatshirt, he pointed into the room, looking at Morgan, who was still at the end of the hallway, keeping her distance. "That's him. That's him. Mini!" he yelled.

"Really? Oh, my gosh," Morgan said, racing up the hall and jogging into the room. It was the chihuahua they had named Toots that, ironically, had the bark of a mastiff. The staff had been unaware of this anomaly until after they had named it. It figured that the noisy little dog belonged to this old trouble-maker.

"Toots, someone's here for you," Morgan said, opening the kennel. Toots shot out before she could catch him. He jumped in the old man's lap and licked him until there was no more spittle left on the old man's jowls. Morgan tried not to grimace. Then the old man, cradling the little dog in his arms like a baby, fed it coke from the liter bottle, tipping it up.

Morgan looked at them both and chuckled. "So, I guess this one is yours," Morgan said, waving her hand toward the little dog. "I see there's no tags. You need to get some identification on him. And he's not neutered. You must do that."

The old man was silent for a few moments, looking as if he was about to croak like a bullfrog, his cheeks all puffing up. "I don't need to do that. Nobody can make me."

Morgan jerked Toots out of his arms, the little dog's bugged-out eyes bulging out even more. "You know what? You can not have your dog," Morgan said, surprising even herself. "He's mine. He doesn't deserve that kind of treatment."

The old man shrugged his shoulders. "I treat him better than I do my grandkids."

Morgan tossed Toots back in the kennel and closed the door on the now-whining dog. "Yes, sir, you probably do, which is also sad. Thank God, I don't take grandkids. However, you violated the law and he was off a leash, running loose. And he's mine now."

"I'll sue your ass."

Morgan smiled, her electric blue eyes flashing like lightning bolts. "Then please sue my ass," she said, pointing to her ass in recently bought thrift store jeans.

The old man started up his wheelchair and flew past Morgan. He was almost to the door when he stopped and spun around. "Could we work out a deal?"

Morgan shook her head to say no but instead said something else entirely. "What kind of deal?"

"I get Mini's nuts cut off and stop filing noise complaints if you give him back to me."

Morgan thought for a moment. "Okay. You have to put an ID on him too and a microchip. And stop poisoning cats."

"Everything but the cats."

"Deal." Morgan had collected all the cats anyway.

Morgan got Toots out of his kennel and gave him back to the old man, who smiled and took the little dog. "Thank you."

"You bet, just please take good care of Toots."

"I will."

"Do you need a leash for him?"

"No, I don't believe in leashes."

"You don't believe in baths either," Morgan muttered under her breath, turning and escorting the old geezer out. Before she even got the shelter door closed, Toots was on the ground and running.

Morgan watched the two fade into the burnt orange Oklahoma sunset, the whir of the wheelchair's grinding and Toots' deep bass barks punctuating the fresh spring air.

Under her breath, Morgan said a prayer.

"Please, Lord, take care of that dog. But you can do what you will with that old bitter man. You got any runaway freight trains hanging around heaven?"

"Ray, hurry up, we've got to go," Morgan said nervously, tucking her little camera into her purse. She stopped to look at herself in the hallway mirror, wondering how to dress when investigating an animal cruelty case. Morgan pulled some lipstick from her purse and applied it on her lips. She puckered up and air kissed, looked at her reflection and wiped off the lipstick again. She pulled dark sunglasses out of her purse and tried those on, too, but she looked too shady, which was not the best look for one trying to look shady-less.

"Ray, what are you wearing to this investigation?" Morgan yelled into the the bedroom.

"I don't know," Ray yelled back. "What do you wear to a PETA investigation?"

"I don't know. I didn't ask and they didn't tell me. Put on your McAfee Mutts t-shirt and some jeans, I guess," Morgan shook her head. "No, put on something that doesn't stand out. Like a black shirt."

"Will do."

"And some black jeans."

"Will do."

The PETA person had only advised Morgan to remain calm when she showed up to investigate the puppy mill owner, who might tell her to get off the property. The investigation would be pretty much over if that happened. Jake and BeBe, the English bulldogs, had both been malnourished, skinny pups, when she rescued them. Morgan reasoned it was from lack of food. But it was dark when Morgan had rescued them, and she hadn't been able to check their food and water availability. But their shelter, Morgan remembered, was hardly that. It was an old cage made of rusty chicken wire propped up on a couple of cement blocks with not even a roof on top. She knew there was a chance that she could shut down this puppy mill, but she would have to be brave and get some photos. She really didn't have a plan, but that was okay. All Morgan's plans of late had gone to dog shit, literally.

"Are you ready?" Ray said, walking into the hallway.

Morgan was still looking at her reflection, wondering who she had become, her scars barely noticeable. "I'm as ready as I'll ever be," Morgan said. She walked toward the door, her dog posse following her every step of the way, and kissed each dog on the nose for luck. She walked out the door to feel the warmth on her skin. The long winter had finally gone somewhere else.

Ray and Morgan climbed into the Dually and headed west on Highway 64 until, a few miles down, they turned south on a country road.

"So, what are our plans?" Ray asked, his wire frame glasses finally resting firmly upon his narrow nose after many office adjustments. Morgan looked out of the truck window onto the river oak trees showing off their lovely ugly in new spring duds. "Didn't you get the memo?" Morgan smiled, the left part of her lip curling down.

Ray laughed. "Humor, from you? Whazzup? Who are you? Are you my wife, Morgan McAfee? Or did aliens invade your beautiful body?"

"Aliens," Morgan answered. "Take me to your leader."

"You are my leader."

Morgan leaned across the wide seat and kissed Ray straight on his lips, Ray contorting his body so he could still see where he was going. "You're in trouble then," Morgan said, grinning.

Ray straightened. "Well, at least we know this woman's got a shotgun," Ray said. She almost shot you with it."

"Yep."

"Well, guess what?" Ray said, pointing under his seat. We got one, too."

"What do you mean?"

"Look under the seat."

Morgan looked under the seat and saw Ray's old 22 that she hadn't seen in a million years. It was the gun he used to hunt with until Morgan had finally persuaded him to stop. It looked a little rusty.

"That's great." Morgan threw up her hands. "We'll all be dead now, and the dogs will be left to fend for themselves."

"Well, then we won't have to worry about the dog food."

They drove for a few more miles, past the beat-up shanties and old rusty car skeletons, until turning in at a trailer house with a black SUV parked in front. Decorating the bare ground was random yard art of women in pantaloons bent over, while several dirty, skinny bulldogs and what looked like big rats, ran up to see what the fuss was about. Not a single tree was anywhere as if the trailer house had been dropped by a tornado straight out of the sky into an open field. Several daffodils bloomed in the flatness, giving Morgan some rare hope.

"You ready?" Ray asked.

"Yep, I guess so."

Ray grabbed Morgan's hand and squeezed it. "Let's see what happens then."

Morgan clutched her purse and opened the door then stepped out, quietly shutting the pick-up door behind her. The big rats weren't that but little dogs, possibly Chinese-Cresteds or some sort of hairless dogs or mangy dogs, the hair fallen out. She tried to pet one but it growled, Morgan backing up a little.

"Hey, who's that?" said a rusty, cigaretted voice.

Morgan looked toward the voice coming from the trailer. A woman, smoking a cigarette, in what Morgan figured one might call a mu-mu, was standing on a plywood platform in front of the trailer. Morgan breathed a sigh of relief, not recognizing the woman.

"Hi, I'm Morgan McAfee and this is my husband Ray," Morgan said slowly as if the woman might possibly be an illegal who didn't understand English.

"We got a call from the People for the Ethical Treatment of Animals..." Morgan said, scared to death, her voice starting to shake.

"You mean PETA," the woman said, spitting out the word like it was a bad pill.

Morgan, looking down and getting nervous, began stubbing out invisible cigarettes in the muddy driveway. "Yes, I mean PETA."

"And what did they say?" the woman asked, sounding as if she might actually care.

"Well, they said they bought a dog from you and the conditions weren't good."

"And who was this person? I haven't sold any dogs in a long time," said the woman, taking a deep puff on the cigarette and exhaling, a smoky cloud around her.

"Well, ma'am, I'm not at liberty to say," Morgan said, choosing her words carefully.

Morgan and Ray were both looking down now, stubbing out invisible cigarettes in the muddy driveway, waiting for her reply, expecting a shotgun blast instead.

"I would be happy for you to see them. Just wait right there for a moment while I change. I treat my dogs like kids."

Morgan, who had been tensing her backside unconsciously, afraid of getting some buckshot blasted into it, wondered how many times she was going to hear this today. She was grateful that she didn't have to shelter kids, too.

She looked at Ray who was looking back at her, his mouth dropping open, a little fly about to buzz into it. "Nothing's this simple," Ray said, shaking his head. "It's the calm before the storm. She must be getting her damned shotgun out." Ray started for the truck. "I better get ours."

"Don't, please, Ray, I'd just as soon she shoot us the way I'm feeling today." Morgan tried to pet the same dog again. It was skittish and backed away from her, but its tail told the real story, it whipping this way and that, the poor thing wanting to be loved. "Come here, cutie pie. Well, those I think are Chinese-Cresteds, Ray. But they look like mutant Chinese-Cresteds, like something out of a bad sci-fi movie. Or *Deliverance*. You know this one looks like Lily. It's got pink skin and a little bit of white hair with black spots, so skinny. Not as pretty as Lily, though," Morgan said, craning her neck and bending over to look at the dog's private parts. "It's a male, though," Morgan said, checking out its belly. "Intact, of course."

"Funny looking, whatever it is," Ray said, his usual critical self.

"I want to put it in my pocketbook," Morgan said, opening her purse and looking inside. I think I have enough room."

"Uh, no."

The trailer door slammed heavy. Morgan wondered how long the woman, who had changed into a jeans and top, had been standing there on the steps listening to them talk. She had also donned huge black sunglasses that were covering her whole face.

"I'll sell you one of those dogs," the woman said, motioning toward the dogs with her long painted red fingernails. "They're China Cresteds. Six hundred. Got the mama and daddy in back. Pretty dogs."

"Oh, we're good. We've got plenty of dogs," Ray said, faking a smile.

Morgan felt dirty like she was in the middle of a drug deal. She was ready to get this whole thing over with. "So you keep them in the back?" Morgan said, craning her neck, trying to get a glimpse behind the trailer house.

"Yep. Most of them," the woman replied, maneuvering down the plywood stairs in high heels, holding onto the rail. "Except for these you see running here. But these are pups."

The woman walked around the trailer, Morgan and Ray following close behind, the woman's stiletto-heels, making a sick, sucking sound, punching holes in the mud. When the smell of feces hit Morgan, the barking and flies so thick, Morgan gagged, not doing that since she had to clean up wormy dog diarrhea the first time.

"I need to clean them up I know," the woman said, her hips crammed in her rhinestone-pocketed jeans, her bangled arms showcasing the puppy mill as if it was a new truck. "I just been out of town a lot."

"Who takes care of them when you're out of town?" Morgan asked, staring back at her reflection in the woman's shiny black glasses.

"I have a guy who does it."

"What kind of dogs do you raise?" Ray asked, trying to get into the conversation.

"English bulldogs and Chinese-Cresteds. I used to raise German shepherds, but these little toy dogs are the bigger sellers now. Plus the poop's not as big. Well, not the Chinese-Cresteds' anyway."

Morgan bent over to look in the first cage. Two bulldogs, a white one that looked just like Jake, and a red-and-white one that looked just like BeBe, were leaning against the wire, looking up at Morgan, their eyes bloodshot. It looked like there was food in the food bowl but their water bowl was empty.

"They look good. Mind if I take a photo?" Morgan said, slowly opening her purse.

The lady stared suspiciously at Morgan with her big black eyes.

Morgan tried to recover. "But they look good. They're very healthy," said Morgan, taking her camera slowly out of her purse. "I've never seen such lovely dogs."

"That's Lucy and Ricky," the woman said, warming. "Great dogs. Had them for years."

Morgan smiled. "They look great. You know these photos that I take can help prove your case. It looks like there's nothing to worry about."

The woman paused, looking at the bulldogs. "Okay. Those dogs are my best friends. They just had puppies."

Morgan tried to act nonchalant and looked around. "So where are their puppies?"

"Oh, they're warm in the house. They're just fine. I've got them on a blanket."

"How old are they?" Morgan asked before thinking better of it.

"Five weeks."

"They probably should be with their mama. That's young."

"Yes, but I wean mine sooner than most. People like them young so they can form a better bond with them."

"Yes, but that's not good socially for a dog," Morgan said before realizing that pups at any age would be better off anywhere but here.

Morgan heard a familiar big bark and turned around. It was Lily, her lovely wispy white tufts ratted and brown, the little dog standing in a rusty cage barely bigger than she.

Morgan felt her heart jump and knocked on her chest to calm it. She walked over, steeling herself from running, and leaned down. "Hey, baby girl," Morgan whispered. Lily licked Morgan through the rusty chicken wire, her little paws, bloody, reaching.

Morgan turned around to face the shiny blackness, trying hard to resist hitting this woman in her stupid, black sunglasses. "How much do you want for this one?" Morgan asked.

"That one's not for sale, but there are others," the lady said dismissively, waving Morgan on to the other barking cages.

"How does a grand sound?" Morgan said, ignoring Ray, his mouth dropped open again.

"Sounds like sold to me," said the woman, walking toward Lily's cage, her shiny hips swinging. "Come on, little feisty one, you're getting out of here."

Beatrice-Chapter 24

At last, after many months of tabling the proposed animal ordinance, the city leaders were up on their platform to take a second vote. Beatrice was so happy that in only two more weeks, after today's vote, the City Council would take its final vote and defeat Blackmon's damned spay/neuter ordinance. Then the entire nightmare would be over.

Tonight, the animal board would make their recommendations, minus the dramatic, agenda-driven Derril Harmon, who had resigned. For the most part, the animal board had nixed the spay/neuter mandate. While waiving a leash law offender's first offense, their second offense fine was cut in half if the offender spayed or neutered their dog. They hoped this would appease Blackmon, who had proposed another one similar to it to the animal board.

Blackmon knew it was dead, so he had left a vestige of it in a leash law violation. The animal board had also tossed out dog breeder restrictions altogether, thank goodness. Beatrice, on the verge of victory, couldn't wait to post the news tonight on the American Dog Club website. In just two more weeks, this would only be a bad memory.

Anne Meyers, gazing haughtily below at Fortville's unwashed, was especially beautiful today with her skin glowing in the fluorescent light.

And Lance Blackmon, his lighthouse eye, temporarily closed with no ships in its sight yet, was smiling his goofy smile, despite his impending defeat.

Beatrice was ready to get these politics behind her. She had a lot on her plate besides Taco Bell lately. Ben and Reba were getting a divorce if Ben could ever find Reba, who had hooked up with a homeless boy (the same one Beatrice had met on the day she had tracked down Reba and Fredo at the park). Dotty would report sightings of Reba and her boyfriend when they showed up at the Homeless Angels for their daily peanut butter sandwiches, but by the time Ben would get there with the divorce papers, Reba would be gone again. Ben also wanted to question Reba about the whereabouts of the prize-winning Lily, the Chinese-Crested that was nowhere to be found. Ben, Beatrice and Dotty had put up "Lost" signs in the neighborhood and posted Facebook alerts but still hadn't heard a thing. But, thankfully, Fredo, Lily's brother, was back home after Beatrice had rescued him. Ben had returned to his kind self, smiling now with new teeth Beatrice had bought for him.

Ben had even shown up tonight in support of Beatrice and was sitting next to her. Dotty, stringing beads, sat next to Beatrice, on the opposite side of Ben. Clingy Dotty had been distant lately.

"Dotty, where do you want to eat after the meeting tonight?" Beatrice asked. Dotty had barely said a word since they sat down.

"Oh, Beatrice, I'm not sure," Dotty, unusually non-committal, replied.

Beatrice tried to be cheerful. "Well, your favorite restaurant is El Cantina. Lets go there and celebrate."

Dotty frowned, still stringing her beads. "That's okay. I think I'll just eat at home tonight."

"Okay," Beatrice said, wondering what she had done wrong.

Mayor Bell called for the animal board to report their findings. Beatrice played Sudoko on her phone as her attention faded in and out of the meeting. Beatrice's blogs hadn't been getting many hits lately, so Beatrice had tamped down the postings. They were going to win anyway. No sense rubbing their faces in it.

"...We also are providing a way for people to license their venomous snakes...." Beatrice heard the new chair of the animal board droning, the she-man who had tried to make eyes at Beatrice at the first meeting. "...So our servicemen will know where the snakes are in case they have to go in there."

Beatrice thought there wasn't a snake within a hundred-mile radius that would bite that woman.

"Thank you for all your hard work, Ms. Smith," Mayor Bell said as the rather rotund woman rolled back into her seat. "Well, we've heard from the animal board, let's take a second vote on the animal ordinance now. Councilman Blackmon, how do you vote?"

Beatrice put her head down, closed her eyes and gritted her teeth implants. She hoped she wouldn't be sick.

"No," Blackmon said.

Beatrice stifled herself from getting up and kicking Blackmon, guessing the animal board hadn't compromised enough for him.

"Councilman Bateman?"

"Nay."

"Councilman Middler?"

"Yes."

"Councilman Fleming."

"Yes."

"Councilman Popodopolis."

"Yes."

"Councilman Meyers?"

"No."

"Councilman Rhodes?"

"Yes."

Beatrice looked up just in time to see Blackmon's left eye flutter.

"Four for and three against," said Mayor Bell. "Clerk, please read the ordinance again in its entirety. And let's take a short break. It'll take awhile."

Beatrice gathered her long, tall self up and walked out into the hallway while Dotty, clutching her craft bag, followed several paces back. Ben followed behind them both.

Seeing Al Nosack getting a drink at the water fountain, Beatrice resisted the urge to push his face into it, but she did not and perused, instead, a historic painting of the first brothel in Fortville and practiced deep breathing exercises she remembered from therapy.

But Nosack walked toward her anyway, his tiny hand extended, oblivious of Beatrice's body language. "Beatrice, hey, how are you?"

"Fine," Beatrice said, still looking at the painting, ignoring his handshake offer.

"So, are you pleased with the animal ordinance?" Nosack asked, not giving up.

"As long as there's nothing in there about making somebody spay or neuter their dogs," Beatrice said, "I'm okay with it."

"Thanks for all you've done," Nosack said, smiling his fake half-smile. "We should get together sometime and talk about politics."

"Yep."

Maybe Nosack, even if he was a snake, perhaps even because *he was a snake*, could help Beatrice with that run for mayor. Beatrice wondered if Nosack was a *registered* poisonous snake.

Beatrice saw Harmon, still in a blasted red shirt, talking to Morgan McAfee. Harmon hadn't left city politics without making a fuss. He had sued the Fortville Humane Society, claiming it didn't walk its dogs enough, and had also gone after Gary Rhodes by filing an ethics complaint, alleging Rhodes with bullying him at the study session. Too bad Beatrice, who loved to shoot whiners, didn't have her invisible guns with her.

And there was that new councilman, John Lowry, who would soon take that spineless councilman Buddy Bateman's place. Lowry had actually won his seat on a no spay/neuter mandate platform. After all the time and energy Beatrice had spent refuting this ludicrous idea, she figured Lowry should pay Beatrice a commission for that campaign idea.

"You let my dogs out!" Beatrice heard, the loud sound ringing her eardrums.

It was the whiny Derril Harmon trying to jump up in Beatrice's face, pointing his finger at her, too short to reach her.

"Derril, don't." It was Morgan McAfee.

Beatrice waved Derril Harmon off with one of her big hands and stepped back. "I did not let your dogs out," Beatrice said, shocked. "I don't even know where you live."

But Derril Harmon kept jumping up in Beatrice's face, pointing at her, both McAfees holding him back now. "I saw it. I saw you following me," Harmon ranted. "A white Prius. You drive a white Prius, Beatrice Cooper."

"Yes, but I would never do that," Beatrice said, Dotty trying to shield big Beatrice but her little body not quite up to the task. "I really could care less about you. Why would I waste my gas?"

"Derril, come on, your dogs are okay. Let's go sit and calm down," Morgan McAfee said, leading him back to the main room. Beatrice saw him glare at her with his big, buggy eyes, his stupid red readers pushed up on his fake black hair, what there was left of the scraggly mess.

"I would never do that, you know that," Beatrice said to Dotty, who was still trying to protect Beatrice, her skinny arms outstretched and scooted up close. Ben, a bit dazed, looked on, not knowing what to do.

Dotty backed off and straightened her self back up, brushing herself off. "I have something to tell you, Beatrice. This may not be the best time, but it's as good as any, I guess. I can't let you take the blame."

"What?" Beatrice asked. Maybe Dotty was finally confessing to feeding Pesto non-sanctioned dog treats.

"I'm the one who let his dogs out."

"*What?*"

Dotty looked up at Beatrice pitifully. "And I had been following Derril Harmon to see where he lived. There weren't late-night visits to Craftmart. I didn't like all the attention you were giving him, writing about him. I mean, I know you had to, but it just made me mad. I was jealous, I guess. It was really awful of me."

Beatrice shook her head while the mayor called everyone back into the boardroom after the second reading of the animal ordinance was complete. Beatrice shrugged her big shoulders and shuffled back in the room. Dotty, her tail tucked, followed close behind Beatrice with Ben behind them both.

"The animal ordinance, minus the spay/neuter mandate, passes on its second vote," announced Mayor Bell.

Beatrice clapped along with the crowd, relief washing over her despite what Dotty had just confessed. Beatrice remembered that Dotty had taken up for Harmon once, making her news all the more confusing.

Blackmon cleared his throat and leaned into his microphone. Beatrice sat down. Dotty and Ben followed suit.

"I'd like to propose an amendment to this animal ordinance that the council had just voted on," Blackmon said, his left eye starting to quiver.

Beatrice felt a deep primal scream down deep in her gut and looked around the room, wondering why people weren't climbing the walls to escape this never-ending nightmare. Poor Gary, sitting right beside Blackmon, was rocking back and forth, tightening his tie around his neck, his mouth tighter than a skeeter's ass.

Blackmon rambled on. "My proposed fines begin on the first offense if the animal is not altered instead of giving them just a warning on the first offense as does the ordinance that was just passed…"

Of course, Meyers and Bateman weighed in, Meyers babbling something about stuff her daddy had taught her like "starting at the beginning of the problem" and Bateman going on about progressivism and how the spay/neuter mandate had been passed in other places.

"First of all, I would like to apologize to Ms. Smith and the animal board for all their hard work on the ordinance," said Gary, who looked as if he was going to self-destruct, his face so red. "But in, in good faith, I cannot possibly okay this."

Meyers called for a motion to vote on the ordinance with Blackmon's amendment. The mayor called the roll.

"Blackmon?"

"Yes."

"Bateman?"

"Yes."

"Middler?"

"No."

"Fleming?"

"No."

"Popodopolis?"

"Yes."

"Meyers?"

"Yes."

"Rhodes?"

"No.

The mayor, who was an old geezer to begin with, looked as if he had just aged ten years. "Four for and three against," he said, shaking his head in disbelief, a forever *Groundhog Day* repeating itself. "Looks like they'll be two more votes on this amended animal ordinance."

Beatrice was in daze. She couldn't believe Popodopolis had flipped. Before this City Council meeting, only one more vote was needed, now two more consecutive votes were left to go because of silly Blackmon's amendment. At least there wasn't a spay/neuter mandate and no dog breeder restrictions in it.

Beatrice waved her big hand at Dotty, trying to get her attention, which startled Dotty, causing her to drop the box of beads to floor. Beatrice tried to smile anyway. "Come on, Dot, let's go home."

"Are you sure?" Dotty asked in disbelief.

"I'm very sure."

Beatrice helped Dotty gather her beads before they walked out into the hallway, where Beatrice saw the new animal board president talking to Blackmon.

"Wait for me in the car, Dot. I've got something to do," Beatrice said, motioning for Dotty to go on out into the parking lot. Beatrice had decided to get a second look at that painting.

"I think you should have taken our board recommendations as is and let us give the first-time leash law offender a warning," Beatrice overhead from the Smith woman, the new animal board president, the she-man. "You had to get your two cents in and push your spay/neuter agenda, didn't you? Well, we, on the animal board were told not to talk about it at all."

Blackmon just stood there taking it, his eye twitching. Beatrice thought this Smith chick had some balls.

In the parking lot, Ben and Beatrice walked together to their cars. Beatrice thanked Ben for coming to support her. Harmon and Morgan McAfee were not far behind them, Beatrice noticed. Beatrice hurried to her car and drove away, Dotty in the passenger side. Beatrice knew she didn't want to bother with Harmon again but wasn't sure at all how she should deal with Dotty now after she had lied.

Lily-Chapter 25

Tiny Mortimer, The Smallest Dog Ever, squeaked while The Biggest Dog Ever clawed at the ground with its big shiny paw and flared nostrils, the horse switching its tail back and forth, watching the boisterous hamster carry on. Behind the Biggest Dog Ever stalked Lily, the little dog crouched low against the sprigs of new grass, trying to be sneaky like her old friend Tom, The Yellow-Striped Skinny Dog. Suddenly, Lily sprang straight up like a bouncy ball and grabbed the tail of The Biggest Dog Ever, seizing its rough strands of hair between her sharp tiny teeth.

The Biggest Dog Ever, surprised and in a bit of shock, leapt forward, Lily dangling on its tail. Mortimer raced behind them both, not sure what else to do, his little legs churning as fast as they could and squeaking for Lily to let go.

But stubborn Lily clenched her jaws even tighter as she went flying through the pasture on her wild ride, swinging back and forth on the tail of The Biggest Dog Ever. She would prove that she, indeed, had the prettier tail and not The Biggest Dog Ever.

"Lily!" It was The Lady with Sad Eyes.

Startled, Lily let go but not before the appaloosa mare soundly kicked the little dog in her fine skull. Lily's body lay lifeless, landing smack dab in a mud hole.

Lily dreamed of Little Mort and Samson tucked somewhere in nice cozy doghouses until she woke up terrified in The Big Noisy Thing.

When Lily saw The Lady with Sad Eyes, the little dog felt better but wondered what she had done wrong. Mortimer and The Biggest Dog Ever were always getting the perfect little dog in trouble.

Morgan-Chapter 26

The river oak trees, the tender buds of spring dotted on their skinny arms, were hopeful. The eastern Oklahoma sky was electric, painted in hot pinks and oranges. The past winter had been especially mean, blowing in not only bad weather but bad politics. Morgan had gotten a wicked dose of both.

Morgan and Ray raced Lily to the vet. Daisy, the appaloosa mare, had just kicked the little dog in the head.

Morgan held Lily in her arms, dabbing with a towel at the gash. "This dog is going to drive me crazy,"

Morgan said turning her head away from the blood-soaked Lily and looking out at the orange morning flying past.

"Hey, you wanted her back," said Ray, shaking his head. "As a matter of fact, as I recall, you *bought* her back."

"I love her spirit. Only a dog could have that. No human could be that resilient and take so many hits. No human that I know anyway."

"I know one," Ray said, smiling and patting Morgan on her shoulder. "And Derril Harmon, too."

Morgan had successfully closed the puppy mill down the road, which was no easy task. Morgan's photos of the bulldogs' empty water bowl and of Lily, so skinny with bleeding cuts on her paws from the chicken wire cage, had sealed the deal. Morgan had proven that the woman in the black sunglasses wasn't taking care of her dogs, so PETA had obtained a warrant for the puppy mill's closure and confiscated the dogs. Morgan had taken all thirty-two dogs and found most of them foster homes, euthanizing only a few that were just too sick.

One of the dogs confiscated from the puppy mill was a long-haired silver Chinese-Crested that she almost euthanized, it so emaciated and sick from parvo. But Lily was his savior, bursting into his kennel as soon as Morgan opened the kennel door. Lily had knocked the poor little dog over and straddled him, his four paws going straight up in the air. She had covered him with kisses, licking his wounds. Lily hadn't left his side until now. Morgan had determined from some records that the dog's name was Sam.

Derril, after resigning from the Fortville animal board, had continued working for the animals. He had filed a complaint against the Fortville Humane Society claiming none of their four-hundred plus animals were adequately walked, which Morgan knew was true. Vice-mayor Rhodes had said the Fortville Humane Society's contract called for "reasonable exercise of animals," so the city attorney rejected Derril's case. Morgan and Derril knew the Fortville shelter dogs were rarely walked since there were never enough volunteers to do it and too many dogs to be walked.

Derril had even batted one out for the humans and filed a complaint with the State Ethics Commission against Rhodes, alleging Rhodes had bullied him at the special session, but the Commission had dismissed the case. Derril hadn't stopped there. He had also started an on-line petition, signed by more than three-thousand people, that had asked individuals to put pressure on the Fortville city officials to insist the Fortville Humane Society follow Humane Society of the United States guidelines. So far, it hadn't gotten much buzz, but Morgan was hopeful someone was listening. At least people were listening in other countries.

Morgan bent over and kissed Lily, who was conscious but woozy in her arms. "I hope she's okay," Morgan said, almost in tears, the shock wearing off and reality setting in. Lily weakly licked Morgan back. Morgan dabbed a little more blood off her wound. "We have to get rid of the horses. We can't keep Lily away from them. She is just lured by them." Morgan shook her head, changing her mind, realizing she couldn't get rid of the horses. "Ray, what about a better fence than the barbed wire instead of getting rid of the horses?"

"It would have to be sort of wooden one or a chain link one," Ray said. "No. That just would cost too much."

"*Please,*" Morgan begged.

Ray smiled and turned into the driveway of Dr. Slater, the Multown vet, whose practice was in a no-frills, yellow-steel fabricated building. He was one of the few vets in the area who still saw large farm animals, although the small, domestic pet business was much more lucrative with far less overhead. Morgan was out of the Dually before Ray even got parked, jumping out with Lily cradled in her arms. She raced into the vet's door.

"Please, I've got to see Dr. Slater," Morgan said to the receptionist on the phone. "The horse kicked Lily."

The receptionist looked up and put her hand over the receiver. "Oh, yes, just a second and I'll get him."

Morgan paced with Lily in her arms until a vet assistant came into the waiting room and motioned Morgan into the exam room, Ray right behind her.

Dr. Slater, a big, pragmatic, no-bullshit type man, didn't greet Morgan when she laid down little Lily on the cold metal table, still dirty from the previous exam. It was no secret that the McAfees weren't Dr. Slater's favorite clients. If Dr. Slater even had any favorite clients, they certainly weren't going to be vegetarian, tree-hugging types.

Lily lay with her tail and feet tucked under her, obviously not her self. "What happened, little one?" Dr. Slater asked the little dog, leaning in and gingerly petting Lily.

Morgan tried to calm down a bit and took a breath. "The horse kicked her. I saw her go flying. It just happened. But maybe the bleeding's stopped." Morgan showed Dr. Slater the blood-soaked towel. "She lost a lot of blood."

Dr. Slater took a look at Lily, examining the small gash on her skull. "Looks like a small concussion. Not much we can do to test a little dog's brain to see if she's okay. But we can help it on the outside anyway. And we can take x-rays to see if any bones are broken."

By the end of the exam and the x-rays, no broken bones had been found and Lily was wagging her tail. She had even started nipping at Dr. Slater, who was not a bit happy about her behavior, and threatened a sedative, which Morgan refused.

After the McAfees checked out, Morgan saw two Chinese-Crested pups, a silver long-haired and a black-and-white-spotted, in the waiting room with a young woman.

Morgan leaned over to pet the pups, forgetting momentarily that Lily was still in her arms, but Lily didn't say a word and only wagged her tail, unusual for the dramatic Lily.

"Where do you get them?" Morgan asked the young woman. "They're so cute."

"Right southwest of here off Highway 64," said the woman, beaming, obviously proud of her two little boys in their matching doggy sweaters. "Lady who sold them to me has English bulldogs, too. These two are brothers."

"Really?" Morgan said, wondering if these pups might be Lily's. Lily had been pregnant when the vet spayed her and aborted her pups. After all, Lily had been gone a little more than six months, which gave her enough time to have a litter. "Well, they're adorable. Take good care of them."

"I certainly will."

Lily's bark on the way out the door confirmed Morgan's thoughts. Morgan smiled, knowing that the world had a little more Lily in it before the guilt came crashing through. There were more than enough dogs in the world already.

Beatrice-Chapter 27

    Beatrice and Dotty were visiting Martina's grave for the first time since the prize-winning Italian greyhound's funeral, nine months and fifteen days ago. The birds were singing their songs and telling the world to get up and get on with life. After all, it was spring. Beatrice was trying her best to resonate. She craned her red-head back upon her thick neck and looked up at the morning sky, the oak tree silhouetted, its limbs ambitious. New leafs tendrils were budding out to see the world despite the crispy leaves still hanging on,

Beatrice amazed by their tenacity, surviving the harshest winter she could remember in Fortville.

She looked at the sun rising and was reminded of how its colors would have reflected upon Martina as her coat changed like a mood ring, differing with every season and its light.

She remembered Martina's black eyes like inky portals that would whisk Beatrice away to kingdoms with Italian greyhounds perched on the laps of monarchs. Beatrice's reflection was halted abruptly by the red dirt pile, bastard paw prints all over it.

Bay-Bay and Rihanna, their bellies bulging out from under matching American flag sweaters crocheted by Dotty, were on leashes in Beatrice's hand. Dotty stood in front of Martina's pink marble headstone, an effigy of Martina atop it. Dotty read from the writings of Marianne Williamson, Dotty's favorite spiritual guru. Bay-Bay and Rihanna had been impregnated by an English bulldog that had somehow gotten into Beatrice's chain-linked backyard. The ever hopeful Dotty was sure the father was Pesto since he was there at the time of the crime.

Beatrice, shaking her head, looked at the wimpy little Pesto at the end of Dotty's leash. Pesto, lacking the fortitude to mate with a drunk watermelon with a hole in it, could not possibly be the father.

Beatrice had sued the bulldog's owner, a bulging, muscular man, for property damage and tried to persuade the police captain to issue a leash law violation. But the police captain hadn't lifted one of his pudgy fingers to help her, which had disappointed Beatrice to such a great extent that she had been rethinking her mayoral campaign.

"The practice of forgiveness is our most important contribution to the healing of the world," Dotty chanted, her palm turned upward toward the pink sky, her frizzy blonde hair backlit by the rising sun. Dotty resembled the saint she had always wanted be, a nimbus of sunlight around her head.

Beatrice had forgiven Dotty for indirectly killing her beloved Martina. It was Dotty's idea, after all, for Martina to be sired by the weak Pesto. His frail offspring had died inside of Martina and taken Martina with them.

This morning, both Big Berta and Ben had come with their dogs to pay their respects to Martina, which had pleased Beatrice. Big Berta, still in her uniform from the late night shift at the factory, held the leash of

Hilda, her Bernese mountain dog. Ben, with little Fredo in his arms, stood next to Big Berta.

The flash of blue around the dogs' necks grounded Beatrice for they were a token of the Coopers' generations of a dog-breeding legacy. Dogs would always be part of the their lives, the family speaking Dog instead of English.

Beatrice had always wondered how Big Berta had come about choosing such a flashy dog collar. It had seemed like such an excessive notion for someone so practical as Big Berta until Beatrice learned the real story.

Big Berta's father, who had raised coon hounds along with twelve children and a wife in a three-room shanty in Tahlequah, Oklahoma, had won a bet on whose dogs could tree the most hounds in two hours. The prize was a light blue leather collar for each of the dogs with "Best Coon Hound" hand-painted on each.

The pink rhinestone letters were added at the suggestion of a Fortville jeweler that Big Berta had dated once. Big Berta loved the way the cheap rhinestones had glittered in the light. Practical Berta initially thought the rhinestones too flashy but changed her mind after seeing the collar on her dog at the time,

Griselda. "Sometimes you gotta splurge on the important things," Big Berta had said. "And my dogs are the important things."

The last vote on the animal ordinance was this Tuesday, and Beatrice had her blog lead all ready to go: *After almost a year of batting the issue around, the bitch, aka the proposed spay/neuter ordinance, forcing one to fix their dog, has finally died.*

Summer

Lily-Chapter 28

The big red sun, low in his sky, was tired from his day of shining and ready for slumber. But Lily was not sleepy, the sun transforming the still pond into a shiny object that beckoned her. Enchanted, the rambunctious Chinese-Crested leapt straight into the water with Sam splashing in behind her. She had never seen this much water all at once, not even in the tall water bowl. Lily ducked her fine head, opened her eyes into the murkiness and plunged back up above the surface to catch her breath. Lily could make out The Lady with Sad Eyes on the bank of the pond but just barely as Lily's head bobbed up and down, her little legs churning under the water. The Lady with Sad Eyes was waving her arms around, yelling, Lily unsure why.

But the little dog, in fine Lily fashion, just ignored her mistress and whipped herself around with her tufted tail and dog-paddled in the opposite direction. *Sam might enjoy a friendly game of tail tag*, she thought. But Sam was nowhere to be found. Instead another Big Black Thing, gouging holes in the water, was headed straight for her, his jaws open wide.

Lily tried to turn and paddle the other way until her world went dark.

When Lily opened her eyes, she was in the paws of The Lady with Sad Eyes, who swatted the little dog's backside with one of them. Lily glared at her though The Lady with Sad Eyes wasn't scared. But Lily thought she should be.

The Lady with Sad Eyes clipped Lily to her belly, where Lily dangled helplessly.

Sam, going on and on, tried to jump up to lick Lily but couldn't jump that high. Lily barked her biggest bark to tell The Lady with Sad Eyes to put her down. But The Lady with Sad Eyes must not have heard her, leaving Lily to bounce around above the yappy dogs, Lily humiliated.

Morgan-Chapter 29

Morgan, Lily and Sam had come to see Derril and two of his dogs for a visit at the Fortville dog park, Morgan taking off some time at work despite Nelda's protestations.

"I swear Derril, I can not let the dog go without her getting into something," Morgan said, wringing the pond water from Lily's topknot, the Chinese-Crested's tufted paws dangling and dripping in the baby carrier attached to Morgan. "I mean, Lily just healed from a cranial concussion, for crying out loud."

Morgan examined Lily's head and neck but didn't see any bites or cuts. A doberman had just lunged for

Lily in the water and grabbed the little dog by the back of the neck but hadn't sustained any damage that Morgan could see.

"You just have to let a dog like that do their own thing. They're never going to be told what to do," Derril said, walking beside Morgan.

Derril stopped and tossed a chew toy out into the parched, golden grass for his newest foster dog, Mouse, the pomeranian at the shelter, and one of his adopted dogs, Sandy, a mousy-brown rat terrier. Sam, pre-occupied and ignoring the fetch game, looked up at Lily strapped into the baby carrier.

"Maybe an obedience class might help her," Morgan said, stepping up her gait, trying to get away from the pond and the doberman. She had just given the doberman's owner a piece of her mind although she wasn't certain if she was in the right since Lily was off her leash at the time of the incident.

"Like you'd even have time for that," Derril said, playfully pushing Morgan on her shoulder causing Morgan to sidestep a little, Morgan almost taking a dive in the pond again.

Morgan grimaced and rolled her eyes, pushing Derril back. "Derril, thanks, I don't need another swim."

McAfee Mutts had moved into their new receiving center after their benefit raised enough money to open the doors. Now volunteers were shooting the shit, literally, instead of picking it up by hand. A brand new high-powered water hose and a state-of-the-art, Ray-designed drainage system with sloping floors were just a couple of the new shelter features. Morgan was hopeful the volunteers, by working in the new shelter, with its more modern, hygienic clean-up methods, would be able to keep an even firmer handle on parvo prevention.

"So, how are you feeling, Derril, after all that happened? With the city?" Morgan looked at Derril and tried to smile while Lily whimpered, winding herself up for a full-on whine.

"You know, I'm okay. I've been so busy," Derril said, bending down and taking the toy from the rat terrier and petting his dogs, worried Sam getting some of Derril's pets too. "I spent some time helping people get reunited with their dogs in that bad tornado in Oklahoma. It was very rewarding. There's still a lot of people I deal with who need help with finding homes for their dogs. I've become quite infamous you know," Derril said and laughed. He was finally able to laugh again after several months of depression. "But you know, all towns have too many animals and not enough homes, it's not just Fortville. And there's drama every where you go. It's not just here. If there's animals and people, there's drama. It's just inevitable."

Morgan bent over and petted a friendly golden retriever that had bounded up, Lily growling. Morgan stood up quickly, jerking up Lily with her. "Derril, did you ever find out who let your dogs out?" Morgan asked, walking quickly away from the retriever.

"No, never did. Had my suspicions, though," Derril smiled, his big green-gray eyes showing signs of life. "But I made damn sure to extract a little revenge myself."

Morgan laughed a bit nervously, afraid to ask, but did anyway. "What did you do?"

Derril smiled big. "Let's just say that Beatrice Cooper might start to take a liking to mutts now."

They both laughed, Morgan unsure if she should be laughing and changed the subject. "Derril, do you think a spay/neuter law would help with the homeless animal overpopulation?"

Derril, shading his eyes from the big setting sun headed south that was lowering itself for slumber, looked out onto the flat horizon. "Eventually, I think, but it's not a quick fix. It would take time. And that would be if everyone in the city was involved, which they are not, obviously. They want easy fixes. There aren't any easy fixes." Derril stopped to pick up the chew toy and pitched it out again for the dogs.

Morgan pushed Lily over and leaned into Derril, linking her arm through his. "Education would be nice," Morgan said. "I've thought about starting in the schools with some of the volunteers, but that takes a lot of resources, volunteers who are available, and most all of us work during school hours. There's only a few retired people who could do it. It's a luxury."

Derril sighed. "Plus, animal welfare work, the actual taking care of the animals, well, it's just hard on your heart. You have to be totally egoless. It's painful to be around a dog that needs a home and may have to be euthanized. Not fun. You want to help and you can't. A single person does not have the resources. It takes a lot of people and resources to pay for the recklessness of other people."

Morgan began to take Lily out of her carrier as they neared the parking lot. Ray was at home doing the dog afternoon chores and Morgan needed to fix him supper and check her e-mail to see if anyone was interested in adopting a dog. Plus, she had to be up early in the morning for work. "Derril, how can anyone be happy when there's so much bad in the world?"

"Oh, but there's so much good in the world that it makes the bad much better. And that would be people like you who continue the fight," Derril said, snapping his dogs on their leashes.

"And people like you, my friend." Morgan hugged Derril and went to clip Lily's leash on her but didn't see her collar. "Oh, Lily's collar's gone. Damn."

"You wanna go back and find it?"

"No, I've got to get home, and I don't want to deal with it now, especially with all those other dogs out there at the pond. That's probably where it is. The dog probably ripped it off her neck when he tried to bite Lily in the water."

Derril glanced back toward the pond. "I'll come back tomorrow and look for it."

"Okay. Derril, thanks for helping the homeless animals. You're a real trooper. You took a lot of hits for them. And were willing to make people think about what's been the usual way of doing things when thousands of animals are dying. That there might be a better way. It's like the Jews at Auschwitz and how people just turned their head while millions were dying. It's dogs instead of people, of course, but the principle is just the same."

    A white Prius passed Morgan and Derril as they made their way in Derril's Range Rover on their way out of the dog park, but neither said a word. It had been a good day, after all.

Beatrice-Chapter 30

It was the end of the long hot summer and the end of the animal ordinance. It had been a year since the animal ordinance had been proposed and debated. The Fortville City Council had approved it four-to-three, getting the final okay on the third reading with Blackmon's proposed amendment, giving leash law or running-at-large offenders a choice to sterilize the intact dog instead of paying a fine.

Gary Rhodes had made a big speech about why he wasn't going to vote for it, but Beatrice was so tired of it, she didn't care anymore. They had, in essence, killed the mandatory sterilization policies for dogs, which was Beatrice's goal. And Beatrice was a bit proud of herself.

Beatrice and Dotty opened the doors to the Prius and let their pack out in the parking lot at the dog park. Pesto came out first, his little feet encased in protective doggy sandals. Next came Rihanna and Bay-Bay, who were followed by Rihanna's offspring: Ciara, a brindle, and Candy, a silver-gray, and Martina, a black-and-white spotted. Beatrice was holding Little Bert, Bay-Bay's sole pup that was always in trouble, white hair growing out in sprouts all over his lean grey-and-white body.

"You know, I just don't see bulldog in those puppies," said Dotty, shaking her frizzy head as she got Pesto's leg weights out of the car. "I still think their Pesto's."

Beatrice looked down at Little Bert, the spitting image of Fredo, and held the pup out for Dotty to examine. "I hate disagree with you, but I think this one, at least, is Fredo's, Dot."

"Nope, I don't think that little horny Chinese-Crested, Fredo, has it in him." Dotty clipped Pesto on his leash and put his leg weights on him, Pesto wincing.

Ben had come by Beatrice's looking for Fredo one day, the little dog gone again, Ben afraid that Reba, still on the run, might have stolen him again. They had found Fredo in Beatrice's backyard but were never sure how Fredo got there. Ben lived only a few blocks from Beatrice, so it wasn't difficult to understand how Fredo could easily arrive at Beatrice's, yet how the dog got in the gate was a question that hadn't been answered. Beatrice, just relieved that Reba hadn't stolen Fredo again, had dropped the suit against the bulldog's owner. After the Fredo incident, Beatrice was unsure whose DNA was running around in those bastard pups.

Dotty, positively glowing, was wearing her patriotic brasier under a blue tank top with short-shorts, the ensemble complemented with red, white and blue tennis shoes. After Pesto had taken a blue ribbon in Kansas City a month ago, she had left the Homeless Angels and opened her own obedience training center.

Beatrice had daringly taken to wearing black cargo pants occasionally. She handed Little Bert a treat out of one of the cargo pockets. The alert little dog took it out of her hand, almost taking a chunk out of one Beatrice's big fingers. "We've got to teach you some manners, little boy," said Beatrice. "Perhaps, I better start by biting you back, you little mongrel."

"Don't call him that," Dotty chided Beatrice. "You'll make him feel bad about himself."

Beatrice chuckled and put Little Bert down near the other dogs, when suddenly, Little Bert took off in the other direction. Beatrice began to run after him, as much as Beatrice could run, but Dotty was already way ahead of her. Bay-Bay, Little Bert's mama, was already ahead of everyone.

"Little Bert, come here!" Dotty yelled, dragging Pesto on a leash beside her. "Beatrice, he's headed for the water."

"I know, I see that," Beatrice yelled from far behind. "Catch him, Dotty!"

Dotty dragged Pesto into the water right behind Little Bert while grabbing for the back of the pup's neck, lunging for him. Bay-Bay was still on the bank, pacing back and forth, afraid of the water. Dotty finally gathered Little Bert but, in doing so, plunged headfirst into the water, while Pesto, high-stepping himself into a frenzy, tried to stay afloat.

But Little Bert was safe and sound above the water, cupped in Dotty's hand. Dotty, laughing hysterically, finally stood up, realizing the water she thought she was drowning in was actually shallow.

"Yay, Dotty," Beatrice said, clapping from the pond bank. "Shake off, good now. Don't want you dripping on me."

While Dotty trudged out of the water, Beatrice saw a flash of blue on the pond bank and walked toward it, wondering what it was. She picked up the blue leather collar with its pink rhinestones and put it in her cargo pocket, looking around the dog park. But there was no little black-and-white spotted Chinese-Crested with pink skin to be found. Her mind flashed to a red Range Rover that they had passed on the way in and Ben's saying something about Reba taking Lily to see a breeder southwest of Multown to sell her.

But that is where Beatrice's thoughts ended, Beatrice needing them to end there.